# LAWS OF EMOTION

# LAWS OF EMOTION

Alison Lohans

*Alison Lohans*
*July 1993*

Thistledown Press Ltd.

Canadian Cataloguing in Publication Data

Lohans, Alison, 1949-

   Laws of emotion

ISBN 1-895449-07-3

I. Title.

PS8573.035L39 1993   jC813'.54   C93-098031-X
PZ7.L63La 1993

Book design by A.M. Forrie
Cover painting by Iris Hauser
Typeset by Thistledown Press Ltd.

Printed and bound in Canada by
Hignell Printing Ltd.
488 Burnell St.
Winnipeg, MB   R3G 2B4

Thistledown Press Ltd.
668 East Place
Saskatoon, Saskatchewan
S7J 2Z5

Acknowledgements

The author wishes to acknowledge several individuals for their
valued input and feedback as these stories developed over
the years: Gillian Richardson, Mary Love, Kathy Kennedy
Tapp, Stewart Raby.
She particularly wishes to thank Seán Virgo, whose discerning
editorial eye helped her to see more clearly.

This book has been published with the assistance of
The Canada Council and the Saskatchewan Arts Board.

*For my sisters*
*Ellen and Kathie, and Robin,*
*my sister-in-law.*

*For my brothers*
*Steve and Brian, and for Ron,*
*my brother-in-law.*

# CONTENTS

# It Wasn't My Fault...

It was all Mr. Baxter's fault.

Not that I happened to be sitting next to Adam Messick at the football game. That was an accident. The way we file into the stands after doing our intro on the field, we often end up sitting next to kids we don't know all that well. So sitting next to Adam was no big deal.

It was Mr. Baxter's fault. Because of the rain.

It was our final game of the season. We had a thrilling record of one win and six losses. The field was soggy because it had rained on and off for several days. Our marching shoes were caked with mud. My best friend Tina Mihalowicz, who was sitting next to me too, had her uniform legs spattered with mud. Out on the playing field our gold-and-white team was rapidly turning brown. And we were getting clobbered. It was only the first quarter.

I felt crummy.

Not because of the way the Cougars were turning us to clowns. Not because of the mud. It had nothing to do with Mr. Baxter. Or Adam.

Tina and I were supposed to be going to the after-game dance. I was devastated. Not because of the dance. But I'd counted on spending some time there with Reilly Higgins — only when I'd been on my way from biology to sixth period English, I'd seen him in the hallway talking to Lisa Morrelli. Not just talking. Looking positively mesmerized was more like it.

I waved and said hi (almost brushing against him), but Reilly never even noticed. I could've melted with humiliation, right into a giant oily spot on the tiles.

Tina nudged me with her trumpet. She has an uncanny way of reading my mind. "Higgins Piggins," she said. "I bet he gets a faceful of mud out there."

"I'll throw it anytime," I offered.

A yell rose up from the other side of the stadium. One of the Cougars was loping toward the goal line. Our number 38 fell flat in the mud. I laughed out loud. Reilly — served the jerk right. The Cougars scored and their pep band blasted out their school song.

One of our drummers tapped out a little competition.

It started raining. Again.

It seemed fitting, considering the way I felt.

The instant the Cougar band quit, Mr. Baxter was snapping his fingers. "Okay, guys — Devastators theme. One, two, one, *hit it!*"

Right away we became a whirlwind of sound. Tina's and my trumpets screamed out high notes. Adam's clarinet shrilled a trill. The percussion section pounded out a throbbing rhythm so catchy I halfway expected to see the whole crowd stand up and start dancing. That was one thing about our band. Our football team might be pathetic. Our field might be muddy. It might be raining — but we were *good* and everybody knew it.

Mr. Baxter had to stop us for the kickoff. One of the drummers played a crescendoing roll as the figures on the field ran slow-motion toward the up-ended ball. Tina's trumpet sang out *Charge!* The crowd roared as the ball shot into the air.

"Mr. B.," said Adam once the game was underway. "It's raining." Mr. Baxter had a way of being impervious to weather. Sometimes I got the feeling he'd keep us playing even if a twister started cleaning off the football field.

Mr. Baxter just smiled pleasantly and pulled his hat down over his ears. "I noticed."

"Oh come on, Derek, you idiot!" Tina shrieked. *"Clobber him!"* And she jumped to her feet, waving her trumpet in the air to help get her point across.

The rain came down harder. It flattened my hair and made cold trickles on my scalp. The stadium lights cast pale pools over the action on the field — only now there was more action and more pools, jillions of jiggly raindrops and multiplying puddles on the track. Already I could imagine how our shoes would squish through them as we marched out for the halftime show.

Tina wiped rain out of her face. "Mr. B.? Are we still doing our halftime show?"

"We shall see," our director said ambiguously. The ranks broke on the football field, and again he was snapping his fingers. "'Peter Gunn.' One-and-two-and-three-and-*GO!*" The trombones and baritones belted out the intro. Tina and I and the other trumpets were ready with our jazzy melody. On the track, Lisa Morrelli and the other rally girls danced in the mud. Their pom poms looked like bundles of wet chicken feathers.

My music was getting soggy. It drooped in my trumpet lyre. Halfway through the piece it wilted completely and did me about as much good as a used Kleenex — but I had the piece memorized anyhow.

Adam wiped the rain off his glasses when we finished. "You should laminate your music, Stacey," he said.

I looked at his. It sat in his lyre, perky as a peacock's tail in full bloom. "Maybe next time," I said.

People in the crowd were grumbling about the rain and paying little attention to the game. The players were all so muddy it was hard to tell which team was which.

"Maybe they'll call off the game," I muttered.

Adam turned to me with mock surprise. His glasses were a blur of wobbling wetness. "Stacey! Where's your school spirit?"

"In the mud."

"Where's your sense of adventure?"

"In the mud," Tina joined in.

"Mr. B.," our drum major said tactfully, "don't you think this much rain is bad for our uniforms? Being wool and all, don't you think they might shrink?"

Mr. Baxter nodded. "The thought had crossed my mind. Okay, troops, fall out. See you back on the spot in street clothes in fifteen minutes."

We let out a huge groan.

In the stands, what was left of the crowd was on its feet, screaming. One of our guys was sloshing toward the goal line, football tucked beneath his arm.

*"Go Eagles!"* Tina screeched, jumping up and down. Her trumpet clipped me on the ear. "Oops. Sorry, Stacey." She grinned apologetically as the player scored our first and only touchdown.

Adam grinned at me too. "Injured?"

"Only my dignity," I murmured, rubbing my ear.

We ambled back to the music room to change. Some kids were furious. "How're we supposed to go to the dance?" a flute player wailed. "Now we won't even have dry clothes to change into."

"Same as everybody else," said Adam. "Dripping wet."

"Oh sure. *They* won't be forced to sit in the rain for two hours."

Tina checked her watch. "Only one hour and twelve minutes now," she commented. "Fifty-seven minutes, by the time we get back."

The girl turned on her. "How come you're on *his* side?"

Tina just grinned and brushed her sopping hair back from her face. "Who said I was?"

"I'm not going back. If he asks where I am, tell him I threw up. Because I will, if I have to sit through one more second of that repulsive game."

In the band room several other deserters were packing up their instruments. Tina looked at me. I looked at her. "Oh what the heck," I said. "I've got nothing to lose."

"Atta girl!" Tina applauded and ushered me into the girls' changing room. It smelled of wet wool and stinky socks. Tina kicked off her muddy marching shoes. "Gross! Where's the air freshener?"

I wiggled into my tights and top. "Don't worry, we'll be getting plenty of fresh air." At least Reilly would be worse off. *He* was muddy — and how would it feel to have rain hammering down on your football helmet all the time? Awful, I hoped.

"Higgins iggins biggins piggins," Tina warned. "You need somebody smarter."

"Like who?" I demanded, poking my arms into my sweater. "Adam?" He just happened to be the first guy to pop into my mind.

"Hm." Tina paused, comb in her stringy hair. "You could do worse."

"No way! I was only kidding. C'mon, aren't you ready?"

Tina pulled on her jacket and blocked the doorway. "Smile, Stacey."

I stuck out my tongue.

Only a few of us straggled back to the stadium. The rain hadn't stopped.

"What're we trying to prove?" grumbled one of the saxophone players.

"That we are individuals of character?" A tuba player explored possibilities of using his huge instrument as an umbrella.

"Shove it, Wallace."

*"Look out!"* Tina screeched.

I looked up. Hurtling toward us from the top of the bleachers was a yellow balloon, obviously filled with something heavier than air. We scattered. My feet slipped in the muck and I fell sideways. Somebody landed on top of me.

"Oh you *guys!*" Tina shrieked with laughter. "You are *too much!*"

Blinking back tears, I tried to extricate myself.

"Sorry about that." Adam got up clumsily. He was drenched with something that smelled like Pepsi. He looked down at himself, then shrugged. "Oh well. It's raining. It'll wash off."

I floundered in the mud. Tina and Adam each extended a hand. "How'm I supposed to go to the dance like *this*?" I wailed.

"Back in a sec," Adam said, taking off at a run toward the concession stands.

"You didn't want to dance with that old Piggins anyway," Tina said fiercely. "Think he'd be a treat, all stinky after the game?"

"*He* gets to take a shower. *He* has clean clothes to change into. And they have hair dryers in the locker room."

Tina giggled. "You could use the guys' locker room."

"Oh shut up."

"Here you go." Adam was back with a huge handful of paper towels. His glasses were so blurred with rain I wondered how he could tell whom to come back to. I felt like a real dipstick as he and Tina and one of the drummers wiped me off. All around us the rain kept hissing down.

Hardly any spectators were left by the time we got back to the bleachers, except a few die-hards who'd had the foresight to bring umbrellas. On the glistening field, brown figures grappled, slithered, fumbled the ball. A yellow school bus had pulled up by the Cougars' bleachers, and a lot of their fans were boarding. Mr. Baxter decided to forget about the halftime show.

"This is *sick*," one of the trombone players groaned.

Mr. Baxter had us play the fight song. Not that it would help. The score was only 49-6, Cougars.

"Mr. B.?" Adam spoke up afterwards. "I can't see my music. I haven't got windshield wipers for my glasses."

Mr. Baxter smiled indulgently. "Then take them off — you've had your music memorized since last month."

"But how'm I supposed to see the game?"

"*What* game?" I muttered.

"Squint," replied Mr. Baxter.

Tina giggled. "Never quits, does he."

I glanced sideways as Adam removed his glasses. His face looked oddly vulnerable, his brown eyes somehow naked, groping to connect with the world.

The game was called off. Rather, we conceded. It was pretty obvious who would win, anyhow.

"So now what're we supposed to do?" I asked Tina as she blew water out of her trumpet. "We can't go to the dance like this. And nobody's home to pick us up." My parents were at a party. Tina's mom worked night shift.

"Hm," said Tina. "We've got a problem."

"I'd give you girls a ride if I had a car," said Adam. His eyes were blinking and his lashes wet with rain.

I had to smile a little.

"We could steal that Porsche," Tina suggested.

I fumbled in my wallet. "I've got ninety-two cents. That wouldn't pay a heck of a lot of taxi fare."

Adam checked the contents of his pockets. "Hey, is that a nickel or a quarter?"

I poked at the coins in his cold hand. "You have seventy-four cents. And a bottle cap."

"I've got two bucks," Tina added.

"The sum total of which would get you girls about six blocks," Adam predicted.

Tina turned on him. "How're *you* getting home?"

Adam shrugged. "Walking. I'm just a wimp. Nobody'd be interested in molesting *me.*"

I looked sharply at him. Was that how he really felt about himself?

Warm air greeted us in the music room. The floor was slick with tracked-in mud. I sat down and put my trumpet in its case. Across the room in the clarinet section Adam looked — well, kind of depressed, as he took his clarinet apart and carefully wiped it dry. I almost felt like going over to talk to him — not that I'd have anything remarkable to say.

Tina charged across the room. "Stacey! Success! Travis said he'd give us a ride."

My stomach somersaulted. Travis had a habit of smashing cars. The two times I'd ridden with him I'd been a mere glob of Jell-O in the back seat. "I guess I'll wait here until the dance is over," I said. "Mr. B'll let me practice or listen to tapes. Or something."

Tina gave me a withering look and followed Travis out the door.

"I'll walk you home, Stacey." Adam's voice startled me.

I looked up. He was still sitting there. I laughed a little. "I live three miles away."

"Oh. Well . . ."

"No, that's okay. But it's sweet of you to offer."

He still hadn't put his glasses back on. Was I just a blur to him? With his hair plastered to his head, he looked like a half-drowned puppy.

"Want to do something while you're waiting for your parents? Get a Coke or something?" Adam got busy polishing his glasses.

It felt weird talking back and forth across the empty room. I went over to sit by him. He put his glasses on. But it was too quiet. I started getting nervous. Why'd Tina have to go off with that drag racer?

I took a deep breath. "I guess we could go for a walk."

A slow smile spread across Adam's face. "A walk in the rain. We're already soaked; what's the difference?"

I grinned at him and got up.

It was glorious walking in the rain. The streets shimmered with light. Water gushed in gutters, sluicing into storm drains. I ran along the wet sidewalks, Adam pounding after me.

"Higgins iggins biggins piggins!" I yelled. It was deliciously satisfying.

"What?" Adam called.

"Nothing." My feet slapped to a halt beneath one of the city's saplings, planted in a dirt square surrounded by sidewalk. I grasped the trunk of the young tree and shook it. Drops cascaded all over me, all over Adam.

"Hey!" he yelped. Laughing, he mopped at his glasses, then gave up and tucked them in his pocket.

Midway between two painted parking stall lines I saw a pinky-greeny-yellowy oil stain. "How pretty!" I said in surprise.

"What's pretty? I can't see a thing without my glasses." Adam grinned and took a turn shaking the tree.

Something went soft inside me. "Can you see *me*?" I asked.

"Oh sure," he said, still smiling. "I can see you with my eyes shut." And then he clammed up.

I watched a traffic light turn green, amber, red again. Cars splashed past, leaving silvery streaks in the street. "Adam?" I said at last.

"Want to get an ice cream cone or something?" he mumbled in a hurry. "They have licorice ice cream at Bailey's."

"Adam." Since he still wasn't looking at me, I had to go stand directly in front of him.

"What?" He wasn't much taller than me, and he looked nervous.

Suddenly I felt on shaky ground. A van rumbled past, spraying water on us. A police car swooshed by in the opposite direction. And the rain kept spattering down, between us, around us, surrounding us. "Adam Messick," I said slowly, "it was really nice of you to wipe that mud off me at the game. And to offer to walk me home."

"It just seemed the right thing, I guess." Rainwater beaded his face. I went a little weak in the knees. I'd never noticed what a nice profile he had.

It was all Mr. Baxter's fault. Mr. Baxter, and the rain. Biggins Piggins Higgins was washed right out of my system. Here I was standing at the corner of Tyrol and Columbia with an unknown quantity.

"Do you *like* licorice ice cream?" that unknown quantity mumbled. "They have double almond mocha too, or just plain vanilla."

I wasn't too sure *what* I liked anymore because everything was swimming in glimmering wetness. "I like licorice."

"Then I'll buy you one." Right away he looked happier.

It sounded like a good buy — especially if he only had seventy-four cents and a bottle cap. I didn't know if I should offer to get him one, too.

"It's a deal," I said, tucking my arm in his.

A heart-stopping smile spread across his face.

It was all Mr. Baxter's fault . . .

# LAWS OF E/MOTION

I was awake until the milkman came.

All night I had lain there, listening to the calls of trains as they slowed for the city which interrupted their relentless charge across the prairies. But there was something about the firm tread of feet upon our front steps, about the gurgling burst of the engine as the truck drove off, that released me into oblivion for a little while.

As always, I was awakened by the roar of the 9:25 flight to Calgary. It was an alarm clock built into me, a hollow ache, a reminder of what had changed forever.

I lay there and tried not to think about it.

The house was silent except for the sound of my spaniel Tiffany snoring in a warm lump nestled against my side. Mom would be at work, and my brother Greg at school. I needed to be at school too, but Mom obviously had decided to let me sleep. The insomnia that had been hounding me ever since Christmas had an ugly way of inviting strep throat if left unchecked for too long.

From my window I watched the silver jet thrusting upward into the milk-blue sky. It disappeared through the gauzy layer of cloud just the way it had the morning Eric left. My throat tightened. I saw, but didn't really see, the diluted sunlight casting its pale glow over tree branches and neighbourhood roofs. Chunky brown house sparrows hopped about on the bare branches. My cat Dominic, sitting on my dresser right next to Eric's picture, began calling to the birds with little chirruping sounds. I stirred. Dominic turned, saw that I was awake, and leapt onto my bed to arch his striped back and rub, purring, against my cheek and outstretched hand.

Now Eric had pneumonia. It was another of many complications.

I was tempted to call him at the hospital, but he never wanted to talk to me anymore. The last time I'd phoned, our conversation consisted of long periods of silence per-meated with the hiss of oxygen and punctuated by monosyllables and agonizing fits of coughing. Eric's coughing, not mine.

The telephone rang. I tore out of bed, scattering the animals, leaving the top sheet trailing on the floor, and dashed into Mom's room to pick up the extension. "Hello?"

But it was only Mom. "You sound out of breath," she said.

"I just woke up." My head and heart pounded from the sudden exertion; at the same time a keen disappointment slashed through me. It *could* have been Eric.

Mom sighed at the other end of the line.

I sprawled out on her bed. Tiffany appeared in the doorway, stretching. "What d'you want?" I muttered when Mom didn't speak.

"I honestly don't know what's best, Tammie." She sounded tense. "I just got a call from your school. You can't keep missing the first two classes each day."

I groaned. "But I didn't get to sleep until the milkman came. Besides, it's just Home Ec and gym."

"And it seems you'll be failing both subjects if you don't start coming to class," Mom retorted.

I lay there and looked stonily at the picture of a smiling me. I hated the girl in that photo. She looked as if only good things could happen to her.

"Tammie —"

"What?"

"I know it's not easy, hon." Suddenly Mom was talking in a rush. "What happened to Eric was tragic. But you're only fifteen, sweetie. Someday you'll find someone else who's just as special, maybe even better. In the meantime there are lots of fun growing-up things to do, lots of people to meet —"

"You're acting like he's dead." My voice went brittle, the way it always did when I talked about him now. Suddenly I hated my mother just as much as I hated the innocent girl in the picture.

Mom sighed. "I'm not going to argue over the phone. See that you get to school in time for third period." The telephone clicked.

I stared at the receiver, then slammed it down. How could she? Half the kids at school talked as if Eric had died, but *my own mother?*

Tiffany sprang onto Mom's bed and I didn't care, even though Mom hated finding dog hairs on the bedspread. At least Tiffany's apricot fur blended well with the mottled golds of the floral spread.

She was wrong, about a lot of things. I was almost sixteen now, not just fifteen. That wasn't so young. And about Eric. Being paralyzed wasn't the same as being dead, not by a long shot. Eric was a once-in-a-lifetime guy; I'd known that the minute I met him.

Megan and I had been in the pedestrian underpass, waiting out a summer thunderstorm, and Eric had burst in, dripping wet and pushing a mountain bike with a flat tire. Something had sparked in the air between us.

Loving somebody didn't stop just because something happened to that person. Or when that person decided he didn't want to see you any more.

Tears came and soaked into Mom's pillow.

I pulled on jeans and my "Life's a Blast" T-shirt, but couldn't face the prospect of school. School was a place where everybody's lives kept going just like always. Everybody's lives but mine — and yet they expected me to think school still mattered.

I took Tiffany for a walk in the gentle April morning. The snow was melting quickly now. Snow. And Eric . . . I pushed it back. I didn't need those images torturing me. Crusted old snow. It was still packed in shady places that never saw direct sunlight, maybe even some of the same snow that was there when Eric . . . I made myself look at the naked brown lawns instead, waiting for the season to turn them green again. Tiffany romped down the back lanes, her stubby tail wobbling in a frenzy as she zig-zagged about, shoving her nose into a dog's paradise of mucky winter leavings.

A bus lumbered past, spraying water and filling the air with stinking fumes. I stared at its mud-spattered back, then urged Tiffany home, at the last minute remembering to wipe her paws. What did they expect, anyhow? I hadn't seen Eric for two whole weeks. I couldn't stand it anymore. It would be good for him to see me. Maybe he'd change his mind.

He lay there motionless. A transparent green oxygen mask was strapped across his face. It gave him an unearthly space monster appearance.

I hesitated in the doorway, wanting to believe it was the wrong room. But I knew better. After a quick indrawn breath, I tiptoed in, waiting for him to notice me.

"Hi," I said, touching his hand.

His eyes were half-open, but he did not respond.

I tried again. "Eric! It's me, Tammie."

He didn't even blink.

A burst of panic galvanized my insides. The only sounds in the room were the incessant hiss of oxygen, and the faint chugging of the machine which monitored every drop of fluid that flowed slowly through the tubing into a vein in Eric's left arm.

"Eric! Wake up!"

He didn't stir. But a long look at the mask was reassuring. Every few seconds it fogged up, tiny droplets condensing on clear green plastic. He was breathing.

I sat there feeling like a strip of crepe paper in cold dishwater. I'd never dreamt he could be so sick. That person in bed was a slack, neglected puppet. Where had *Eric* gone, the guy who used to ski along the cross-country trails, laughing back at me when I couldn't keep up? Who had a magical way of short-circuiting the world when he looked at me?

It had to be a terrible mistake. And yet, like all those other times, I knew it wasn't.

"This isn't a good time to visit."

I jumped and glanced at the nursing assistant who'd just walked in. Sharp-eyed and carefully manicured, she wasn't one I recognized. "Can't I just sit here a few minutes? I haven't seen him for ages, and I won't bother him." There were lots of things I needed to ask, but I had the feeling she wouldn't listen.

I watched her wrap a blood pressure cuff around Eric's limp arm, squeeze the black bulb to inflate it, then listen through her stethoscope. Without further comment she slipped out of the room on silent feet.

"Eric!" I whispered. *"Please,* wake up!" I shook his shoulder.

His eyelashes fluttered; his grey eyes focused on me at last. "Who are you?" His voice was so faint behind the oxygen mask that I had to bend very close to hear.

Pain knifed me. How could he *forget?* "You know me. I'm Tammie."

"Oh. Tammie. Nice to meet . . ." His voice faded and his eyelids drooped once again.

"Eric! Don't fall asleep. It's me. *Talk to me!"*

His eyes flickered open, dull and confused. "Is it time to go already? Can . . ." His voice trailed off as he reached into the empty air above his head, groping for something that wasn't there. Beneath the sheets his legs did not move.

"Eric." Warm tears spread across my cheeks.

"Go away!" he said in sudden irritation. "I don't want any." But he was looking at the ceiling, not me.

I tugged at his hand. "Eric."

His blank eyes met mine. "Nurse, it spilled."

I had to fight back the panic. "You're not making sense," I choked. "Can't you try to make sense?"

"She's crying," he said in a shuddery whisper. "Grandma, could you take her home?"

His grandmother was nowhere in sight. But a nurse waited in the doorway, an older black woman. "He's been pretty confused," she said in a low voice.

"How come?" Words wanted to spew out like a scattering of dried cat food. I swallowed hard.

She came in and studied the chart at the foot of Eric's bed, her face sombre. "He's hallucinating a lot. His brain isn't getting enough oxygen, you see." She looked at me then; her knowing eyes were liquid with compassion and for an instant I wished I could cry against her bosom. Her name tag read "Muriel Parsons, R.N."

"He'll come out of it, don't you worry." She smiled, and then turned to Eric. "Eric, honey, are you breathing any easier now?"

His eyes had drifted shut again. He didn't answer.

I ached. "How'd he get pneumonia?" I asked, tracing my finger in loops across the front cover of a *Sports Illustrated* that lay on the bedside table. It was something I'd never understood.

The nurse, Mrs. Parsons, explained, ending with another "you see", but my mind was buzzing like static and I didn't see, not at all.

I nodded anyway, then walked out, suddenly too numb to feel anything. With a startling clarity I realized that at school it was mid-morning break, and Megan would be waiting by my locker, wondering where I was.

In an odd way I felt like Dominic, trapped behind the glass windows that kept him from the birds. I was behind glass too, somehow, thick glass, nearly soundproofed.

Somehow I ended up on a bus. Somehow I got off at the pharmacy where Mom worked.

I went to the back of the store and sat down on the chair by her druggist's counter. It was safest to look at the blue-and-green flowers on the carpet.

"What's wrong, Tammie?"

It may have been the second time she said it. At last her voice penetrated the silence enshrouding me. I looked at her but couldn't talk, couldn't connect images with words.

"Tammie! Are you all right?" Now her voice was sharp and worried. Her pill counting spatula clattered against a bottle of yellow pills.

All I could do was shrug and look helplessly at her.

She came around the counter and knelt directly in front of me, looking me in the eye. "Tell me, sweetie."

"Eric." At last something came out. It was mostly a squeak.

Something like anger snapped in Mom's brown eyes. Then suddenly she had me gathered into a hug. "Oh baby, baby," she murmured, rocking me gently. "I'm *so* sorry."

I had to struggle to talk. "He's not —" The words were little chips of sawdust. "He — he —" The glass cage around me cracked, shattered into thousands of splinters, and the world was all raucous noise.

Mom pulled back, puzzled. I was crying again and couldn't explain.

She sighed. "Why didn't you go to school?"

My answers sounded silly. It was as if Eric's mixed-up condition had somehow seeped into me. The harder I tried, the worse it got.

She shook her head. "I think it's time we called —" She broke off as a woman walked in with a prescription and a sobbing child. All white-coated efficiency, Mom whisked back behind her counter and went to work.

I wiped my eyes and stood up so the customer could have the chair. I'd heard it all before, anyhow. How Mom thought I was too hung up on Eric, and wanted me to see a shrink. But I couldn't help the way I felt.

After a minute or so I sensed the woman sneaking glances in my direction. As if I were contagious. Or on a drug trip. It irked me.

"I'll call you from school, Mom," I said. Holding myself straight, I left the drugstore. I could feel her wanting to chase after me.

School was the best place to go. I could lose myself in the bustling activity and maybe forget, for a little while. Home Ec and gym were over. Too bad; I'd have to make sure I showed up tomorrow. English would be getting out when I got there, and I'd meet Megan for lunch. Then we had physics. Mme Genereux had said we'd be using gyroscopes in lab. Something about laws of motion. I'd be working with Megan and Chris . . .

Laws of motion.

I caught the next bus and swayed with its motion. The morning jet had followed its plotted course, heading steadily westward. Just like the jet that carried Eric and his family to the Rockies over Christmas holidays. Eric's family, and their skis . . .

I shuddered and thought of Tiffany, on the walk this morning. She'd obeyed her instincts, moving around, exploring the uncovered earth after its long winter sleep. Eric, so terribly sick, was in a private world that nobody else could see into. But what about me, Tammie? Was I supposed to be spun completely off course because of Eric? We weren't the same person, he and I. And as Mom had said, I was only fifteen . . .

At last the fear inside had dulled. A new kind of quietness was budding, not masking the fear, really, but waiting patiently beside it. Eric had been in hospital three months now.

I blinked, seeing again the images that haunted me any time I lay in bed, trying to sleep. Eric. Skiing. Grinning, in his new blue-and-green-and-white ski outfit. Losing control. On a steep slope. Falling . . . My mind showed me clearly, no matter that I hadn't been there to see. Snow flying, skis and poles flying, Eric flying . . . flying, flying, rushing to meet that tree.

He wasn't likely to come home for a while.

Whatever happened, I was still Tammie. I'd have to keep right on going. In my own way, toward whatever was yet to come.

I pulled the cord. The bus slowed.

# THE MICHELLE I KNOW

Rob was late. And last night he'd gone to the after-game dance. With Vanessa.

Michelle turned over. The hospital bed was hard and confining. The entire back of her neck felt like one giant pillow crease. She rubbed it and as always, her fingers crept upward to explore the terrifying bleak landscape where her hair was supposed to be. She didn't have the energy to pound the pillow good and hard. Even if she did, she'd probably knock the intravenous needle out of place and then she'd have to lie there gritting her teeth while nurses poked and jabbed to set another IV.

It wasn't fair. Sometimes she felt so tired and sick it was even hard to lift the remote control for the TV.

Her clock radio said it was 7:27. Maybe Rob wasn't coming. She wasn't much to come to. Not any more. Even after the other kids quit showing up, he'd stuck it out. Once he'd even smuggled in his mom's poodle pup to break the monotony. But now maybe he was having second thoughts.

All Michelle could see outside the fourth storey window was cottony orange light dissolving into darkness. In the distance a siren screamed, drew nearer, then passed beneath her window. If she got up, she'd see blood-red lights flashing below and people hurrying into Emergency, all softened by the winter fog. Sometimes the fog got so thick it looked like you could walk right out the window and keep on going. Michelle's mouth quirked. In reality, it would be more like plunging down — gown flapping about her, IV monitor and pole and bottles all set to smash on the sidewalk. How much would it hurt, before . . ? But that might be a quick escape.

The guitar started playing again. Michelle relaxed a bit and fidgeted with her earrings. One of the holes in her left ear was kind of sore. She sighed and took out the tiny purple triangle, feeling for a safe spot on the bedside table. If her earlobe got infected, Dr. Warkentin would give her major heck.

She closed her eyes and tried to let the music wash away her frustration. It was total boredom, being in hospital for almost two months. Probably she was turning into a turnip. Or some kind of squash. No wonder Rob wasn't here. Vegetables weren't the greatest company. At least the music made everything more bearable. This was the third day. Or was it only the second? Time got pretty blurry, cut off from her normal life.

The soft scuff of rubber soles on carpet, the faintest swish of clothing, told her that Brenda, the evening nurse, had come in. "Hi, kiddo," came the cheery voice. "Anything I can do for you?"

Eyes still shut, Michelle shook her head. She'd had it with hospitals. With routines. Needles in her arms. Chemotherapy that left her feeling like something a pulp mill spat out.

Brenda's voice prodded at her. "Your friend's late."

Michelle looked dully at the young nurse. "I don't think he's coming."

"Oh hush!" Briskly the older girl straightened the untouched pile of magazines left by the occupational therapist.

"I bet —"

"Watch out for my earring." Michelle tensed, then heard the predictable *thkk* sound of a tiny object hitting the carpet.

"Sorry." Brenda stooped. "I'll put it in your top drawer, okay? Now. Your friend. I bet the fog's keeping him. When I went out at supper it was like walking through whipped cream."

Michelle smiled faintly and waited while Brenda took her pulse and temperature, then checked the drip from her IV bottle.

Brenda patted her hand. "Cheer up. Doctor says your blood counts are super. You're on your way to remission, kid, and you know what that means."

"Yeah," she said sourly. "I get to go home and wait six months before I have enough hair to do anything with." It would be heaven to go home, though. It seemed ages since she'd been *someone,* with thick dark hair that swished against her cheeks. Who had lots of friends, and clothes that fit right. Who felt like the world was hers.

Now it was safest not to hope.

Brenda tossed her straw-coloured braid over her shoulder, then placed her hands in her uniform pockets. "You'll feel lots better once you're home. But you may not want to leave us . . ." The nurse's voice lowered. "You've got an admirer right here in our midst, and *he* thinks you're gorgeous."

"Yeah, right. Tell me another one." Michelle shifted and the IV pole rattled.

"Honest. It sure isn't me." Brenda indicated her comfortably padded waistline. "If I ever get a boyfriend I'll know I'm dreaming."

"At least you've got hair." What she really meant was that Brenda had a face that was . . . friendly. The kind that was sure to draw people to her — but it would sound pretty sucky to say it out loud.

"So have you," Brenda countered. "Where is it, stuffed in the drawer with your washbasin?"

To be exact, the wig was stuffed in the drawer *under* the washbasin. Mom bought it when her hair first started thinning. It was awful. The colour was right, but that was all. Any way you looked at it, it was fake hair — like what you'd see on a Barbie doll.

Michelle glared at her skinny arms, mottled with bruises and needle scars. "It's gross," she muttered. "It's too hot. And prickly. Who cares, anyhow, with a death sentence hanging over your head?"

Brenda swished across the room to get a handful of clean straws from the cabinet. "Cases like yours go into remission for years now, Michelle," she said firmly. The way she said it, it sounded like she knew exactly how it felt to lie there at 3 a.m., scared cold, and faking sleep as the night shift crept in with flashlights to check the IV and write on the chart. "We had the cutest little guy in here once — he never came back, so we all started thinking maybe he didn't make it. But Doctor says she sees him every now and then, skateboarding and riding his bike like a maniac."

Michelle fell silent. In the hallway came the clatter of rolling wheels. Sour-faced Mrs. Begbie paused in the doorway, leaning heavily on her IV pole, her own bald head covered by a turquoise hat with wild feathers. "Nurse," she wheezed, "can you get someone to bring my pain shot?"

Brenda glanced at her watch. "I'll go check on it for you, Mrs. B."

Bored, Michelle flicked the TV switch. But that drowned out the guitar. She flicked it off and the screen went blank. Just like she felt. Visiting hours were almost over. Rob wasn't coming.

Suddenly Brenda was back. "C'mon — I'll take you to see Claude. Your admirer. Keep your friend guessing a little, huh?"

Michelle inspected the cool clear tubing that fed sugar water and, sometimes, chemo into her arm. "I don't feel like it."

"C'mon, go for it! Put on your wig — you can model it for Dr. Hernandez. He's at the nursing station."

Michelle groaned, then sat up because there was nothing better to do. But she left the wig in the drawer. "This Claude. Is he bald like me?"

"Right on. And he thinks you're gorgeous."

"Oh sure." Wearily Michelle swung her legs over the edge of the bed and let Brenda put slippers on for her. Her knees were bony. And the skimpy hospital gown was too much — even a mannequin would drop dead wearing it. She slid one arm into the hot-pink dressing gown Brenda held ready, but even that looked gimpy with one sleeve dangling because of the IV.

"Glamour!" Brenda's eyes teased her.

"God. What'd you do with my mink, throw it down the laundry chute?"

"Yep." Brenda's strong arm came around Michelle's waist as she pushed up, grasping the IV pole. "And I'm afraid I've got some bad news. It shrank."

Dr. Hernandez, the young resident, looked up and waved as they inched down the hallway. Michelle waved back, then remembered. Rob hadn't come.

"And here's Claude."

Michelle took one look and wished she could turn and run. Except she was too tired.

Claude was old enough to be her father. His arms were bruised like her own. His bald head gleamed with shiny flesh. A guitar lay in his lap.

Dizzy with exhaustion, Michelle sank into a visitor's chair. Some admirer. What was he, a dirty old man? See if she ever listened to Brenda again!

"So you're Michelle."

"Yeah," she mumbled and looked away.

"We're all pretty proud of Claude," Brenda said. "He's been in and out of this place for eight years now, and each time he comes back, we learn something new."

Eight *years*? And she'd thought eight weeks was torture. "I can hear you in my room," Michelle said hesitantly, since they obviously expected her to talk. "It helps."

Light glowed in the man's dark eyes, and suddenly his face was beautiful. "I taught myself to play in this joint," he said. "Drove everybody nuts." His right hand, splinted to keep the IV needle in place, strummed the guitar with a caressing stroke. A flurry of notes scattered.

"You?" said Brenda. "Never."

Outside a train rumbled past. Michelle fell silent. Ironic how hospitals ended up in the noisiest parts of town. Ironic how she, once with everything going for her, had so quickly been thrust on a shelf, forgotten, and now by Rob too. Once cancer cells got their claws into you, none of the old rules applied. You were totally at the mercy of doctors and nurses. And the disease.

"It's not so easy, eh?" Claude's soft voice startled her.

Quickly she forced her face into a polite mask. No point in grasping for the sympathy of somebody just as sick — probably forty, and bald besides. Brenda had disappeared; she guessed it was either be polite and talk, or else try getting back on her own. "No," she said. There was a long pause. Claude's bound fingers gently plucked the guitar. "You've had leukemia for eight *years?*" she burst out.

"Eight years. A long time. It's been pretty hard on the family. But I'm lucky. Most patients my age don't last."

Michelle looked cautiously at Claude, whose shiny bald head had odd bumps and ridges just like hers, who lacked eyelashes and eyebrows. Just as she did. "Do you ever feel like–" She broke off, then barged ahead after a steadying breath: "Like sometimes you'd rather die than be poked by one more needle?"

Claude looked beyond her, out at the night sky. "Sometimes," he said at last. "But we were each given a life. You don't throw that out like garbage."

"I hate it!" Sudden tears trickled down Michelle's cheeks and she wiped at them furiously. "How I look. How I feel. I hate *everything!*" She sniffed hard, blew her nose, but couldn't stop.

"Yeah, it gets that way sometimes." Claude's fingers coaxed more notes out of the guitar, sending music spilling into the hallway. Michelle rested her cheek against the ridge of the bedside table. "I've been there," he went on. "But you know, we're all in this together."

"Not my friends," she said bitterly.

"You have to be strong inside," he said. "Don't waste yourself fighting the wrong things."

Michelle traced her fingertip along the hard tabletop. At least this man was better than sour Mrs. Begbie, or Mr. Morris who let himself be wheeled around like a big doll. This man had dignity. Did she?

"Michelle?" Brenda's voice penetrated. "I found this guy wandering around the hallway. Is he somebody you know?"

Rob! He stood there in the doorway, still bundled up in his jacket, his face tense.

With a great effort Michelle wiped her eyes. "Hi," she mumbled.

The music stopped. A warm hand rested on her shoulder. "Remember. You've got to fight it."

She managed a wan smile. "Yeah."

"Sorry I'm late," Rob said. "That fog's impossible. I practically had to get out and put my nose on the street just to see the lines."

"Your attention please." The cold voice of the intercom spoke with dismissive finality. "Visiting hours are now over."

"Shush!" Brenda waved her hand at the speaker in the ceiling. "Quick! To your room!"

Shakily Michelle stood up, leaning on her IV pole. Rob moved in to help her. He smelled like fresh air. Which meant she must smell like . . . the hospital. Sick. Grimly she kept her legs moving and her grip tight on the pole; she'd already learned how hard it could be to get back up after a fall. But visiting hours were over, and now Rob would have to go. Her eyes blurred.

"Who was that guy?" Rob asked.

"He's been sick for eight years." She knew she was wobbly, but it felt as if Rob had just shuddered. Walking took so much of her energy that she couldn't say more. Her bed, freshly made up, looked like heaven. Wearily she sank onto it.

But Brenda was drawing the curtains around her. Rob was pulling up a chair. "She says I can stay half an hour if I promise to be good," he whispered.

Brenda winked and disappeared.

Suddenly Michelle didn't know what to say. Here was Rob, late because of the fog. But his face was still tense and his eyes were guarded. "How was last night?" she mumbled.

"Okay," he said indifferently. "We won the game."

They were not on the same wavelength. Needing to be doing something, Michelle reached for her mirror and studied herself. Her shiny bald head, the bony ridges where her eyebrows had once been. She yanked the wig out of the drawer and pulled it on. Loose hairs caught in her right earring. Furtively she glanced at Rob. "Well?" she demanded. "Am I still ugly?"

Rob sighed.

Might as well forget it. Who wanted a bald girlfriend who couldn't do anything but cry? "I'm ugly compared to Vanessa." She couldn't help the waspish note that sliced into her voice.

"What's the deal about Vanessa?" Rob's fingers tensed as they dangled between his knees. "I only went for something to do. Vanessa's boring, okay? The whole stupid dance was boring. What else do you want to know, what we —"

"Sorry." She felt heat creeping into her face. "When you were so late, I guess I thought . . ." Out of the corner of her eye she watched him. His jaw was tight, but his green eyes were intent on her. "And then because I'm so ugly and everything, I thought . . . Oh forget it!" She pulled the wig off and threw it. It landed on her IV bottle and dangled there rakishly.

Michelle bit her lip. It looked so awful she nearly cried — to think she'd hoped Rob might like her better with the wig on. But it didn't look just awful, it looked — *awful*. So awful that . . . A giggle escaped.

Suddenly Rob lurched to his feet. He bowed to the IV pole. "Allow me, madam, may I have this dance?"

Michelle laughed out loud.

Rob grinned.

Michelle clapped a hand over her mouth, trying to keep her voice down, for suddenly she couldn't stop laughing. But she couldn't let herself get carried away. It was all very well for noble Rob to come to the hospital every day to see poor Michelle, who was so sick with leukemia, *but* . . .

"You shouldn't feel like you have to come here all the time," she mumbled. "It's no fun for you. I mean, you've been fantastic, really fantastic, but I don't want you to start hating me because I'm such a . . . " She swallowed hard.

Rob had to be set free. It wasn't fair to expect him to be the knight in shining armour. She had to have the strength to let him go.

"Michelle." His voice was quiet; solemnly he lifted a few strands of hair from the wig, rubbing them between his thumb and fingertips. "What we've got — it's based on a little more than hair, you know?"

She hiccupped, hardly daring to believe what she was hearing. She had to change gears, fast. Deliberately she rubbed her hand over her bald head. "Well, at least this never gets tangled." She gulped in a deep breath. "How do you think it would look with flowers painted on it?"

Miraculously, Rob was still there. He was even laughing, and his incredible, world-stopping grin was dawning in his eyes. For the first time in months, Michelle felt a real smile swelling inside.

"Now *that's* the Michelle I know," Rob murmured. He leaned closer.

# TO TOUCH A SHADOW

Three weeks of music camp. A long string of letters afterwards. Emily never dared to hope for more.

But then Joshua called to say he was coming.

"Quit being so *nice*," Scott had said as they sat in the orchard. "When will you learn to say no?" His keen grey eyes studied her, shaming her.

Emily hung her head. She felt silly talking about Joshua with Scott.

It was hot, even at dusk. Curling peach leaves cast them into shadow; the air was heady-sweet with the scent of ripe fruit. A noisy frog chorus sang in the irrigation ditch nearby, a bullfrog keeping time with its rusty, booming bass.

"I wish you weren't going," Emily said.

"*What?*" Scott laughed. "Skip the deep-sea fishing trip just to meet your friend?" But then he caught her hand. "Should I worry?"

"No." Emily's cheeks prickled. She'd been mesmerized by Joshua, but he apparently thought of her as a good friend, nothing more. After camp he'd gone back home to San Diego, three hundred miles away, and that was that. Except for the letters. She'd been so excited at hearing his voice on the phone it wasn't until later she realized the dilemma. Did Josh know some things had changed? She'd mentioned Scott. Hadn't she?

Scott glanced at his watch. "I've gotta go pretty soon. The plane leaves at eleven." A faraway look crept into his eyes. "San Diego tonight, and then . . ."

A mosquito was whining around Emily's ear, and she missed the rest of what Scott said. She cuffed at the bloodthirsty pest, missed. "Ow!"

Scott laughed.

"Off with your head!" Grinning, Emily reached for a fallen twig. *"En garde!"*

Scott found his own weapon and they clashed swords. At the slightest pressure, the brittle sticks snapped.

Emily fell back laughing. A moment later she was breathless because Scott was kissing her. But in the back of her mind a voice was prodding. What was she going to do about Joshua? After all, she had a whole drawerful of letters signed *love, Josh.* Letters she'd answered with *love, Emily.* In spite of Scott.

"Hey!" Scott said. "You out in space?"

Emily smiled. Scott straightened up. "Tomorrow I'll be out on the water," he said dreamily. *"Man,* the fish! Want me to bring you one?"

"Like a bouquet?" Emily smothered a giggle at the thought of a fish elegantly wrapped with ribbons and a card — plus roses, for the effect.

But then she sobered. Why couldn't Scott and Josh trade places?

It would never work, though. They were so very different. Into heavy metal and motor cycles — and fishing — Scott was a wiry guy who never sat still for long. Josh, a serious music student, played saxophone with an intensity that could quiet even a roomful of loudmouth junior high school kids.

"C'mere." Scott tugged at her.

For a few minutes everything drifted. Until a shrill beeping jolted them.

"Oops!" Scott slapped at the alarm on his watch. "Gotta run. Dad'll kill me if I'm late."

"Have a good time," Emily said wistfully.

Scott straddled his Yamaha, a sure foot kicking the beast to a fury. "Hey!" he yelled over the noise. "Don't catch any big ones while I'm gone, huh?"

She let out an exaggerated, long-suffering sigh. "In the *ditch?*" But Scott probably didn't hear as he swooped away.

The lights of home reached through the orchard, yellow and welcoming. Shrieks and splashing came from the pool where her younger sister was entertaining friends.

But it was too soon to go back. Moodily she sat on the irrigation weir, a small concrete bridge damming the ditch. With a hollow roar, water rushed over two boards in a miniature cataract. After a listening stillness, one frog began croaking again, soon joined by dozens of others. All around lingered the smells of water and earth and ripe peaches.

"Rats!" she muttered, flinging a stick into the ditch, once again silencing the frogs. Caught in the current, the stick hesitated, then skimmed over the boards and away. Heading south. Toward San Diego.

"*Rats!*" she said again. She might as well run away to Nebraska.

She went home. With shaking fingers she dialed a number in the 619 area code. Four rings. No answer. Eight rings. Still no answer. Thirteen rings. Numbly she sat there listening to the telephone ringing in Joshua's house.

At last she hung up and went to her room, where she picked up the gilt-edged photo of Scott which sat on her dresser. She studied the rugged contours of his face, his direct grey eyes. Joshua's eyes were like that. Honest.

Memories of music camp were shadowy and elusive, hard to trust anymore. Wading in the creek, frigid water splashing through her rolled up jeans -- and catching Josh's hand for support. Trying to steal third base in a softball game — and Josh, at second, grabbing her around the waist and holding her back, to the mirth and indignation of the girls in her cabin. Whispering and laughing in the camp office, and finally, once they'd regained control of themselves, playing "Taps" through the PA system, he on a length of garden hose, and she on a set of carefully-tuned drinking glasses. The last night, standing on the deck with the wind sighing in the pines, when Joshua had almost kissed her. She savoured the memory. But he hadn't kissed her. And she'd been a little mad at him ever since.

Quickly she opened the drawer stuffed full of letters. "You goof, Josh!" she muttered. "You never even sent me a picture."

\* \* \* \*

The air conditioner quit the next morning. By one in the afternoon the thermometer outside had climbed to a sizzling one hundred and eleven degrees.

"What did we ever do to deserve this?" Emily's mother moaned, sipping iced tea while an electric fan probed ineffectually at the stifling air.

Emily sat there with perspiration dribbling down her back. "Poor Josh," she said. "Coming on a day like this. I hope he's got air conditioning in his car."

Her mother turned to look seriously at her. "He's a nice boy, this Joshua? He won't expect—"

*"Mother!"* Emily shrieked. "He's not like that." She stomped out. To her dismay, her eyes pricked with tears.

The searing heat nearly put blisters on the soles of her feet as she crossed the patio. She plunged them into the tepid pool. All around her the air was like a blast furnace. Fully clothed, she slid into the water. Josh wasn't due for at least another hour; she'd have plenty of time to change.

But a sudden shout told her otherwise.

"Emileeee!" There was a delighted laugh, and Joshua came loping across the lawn. The sun gleamed off his longish almost-black hair.

Sheepishly Emily scrambled out of the pool. "You're early!"

He swung her around in an exuberant hug. "It's so good to see you!"

Dizzily she rested her hands on Joshua's arms, then her head against his shoulder as he pulled her closer. He smelled faintly of after-shave and spearmint gum, and seemed taller than last summer, more solidly built — but then he ought to; he'd just turned eighteen. Or maybe the dazzling sunlight was making her woozy. Trembling, she pulled back a bit. "Josh, I've got to tell you —"

His brown eyes, flecked with green, smiled down at her. "That you've gotten me all wet?"

She sputtered with laughter and relief. "It's your own silly fault!"

His eyes sparked. "And so's this." He scooped her up and tossed her back into the pool.

She shrieked. Water closed over her. Well away from the edge, she surfaced. "Some way to treat your hostess!"

He grinned, emptied his pockets, pulled off his sandals, then his T-shirt. He dived in. An instant later something seized her heel, yanking her under. In the green sun-spangled world, surrounded by silvery bubbles, she looked at Joshua's watery image. Then she shot to the surface, bursting with stale air.

Joshua came up beside her, grinning in a way that made her insides quiver. But he didn't kiss her. Scott would have.

She had to say something.

But not yet; he'd just driven three hundred miles on the hottest day of the year. Did he even have a change of clothes?

Emily hoisted herself out of the pool. "You sure got here fast. What'd you do, speed all the way?"

Sloshing a miniature wave across the concrete, Josh sat beside her, his tanned legs stirring the water gently. "I left early — I drove up to Glendale last night, and stayed with my cousin."

"No wonder. I didn't even hear your car drive up."

"Haven't *seen* it either." Pride rang in Joshua's voice. He held out his hand — but only to help her up. They walked around the house to the driveway, through the shadow cast by the peach orchard, their feet suddenly white with dust. He didn't reach for her hand again. Scott would have.

Emily shivered despite the overwhelming heat. And then she stopped short at the sight of a Toyota completely covered with abstract musical designs. "Oh *Josh!*" she cried.

He smiled. "Painted it myself. Want to drive around? It's air conditioned."

She hung back. A car like that would catch the eye of every kid in town. For Scott's sake, it would be kinder to keep a low profile. "Maybe later."

He drooped a little.

Panic nibbled her insides. What could they *do* for two whole days? Tiptoeing gingerly across the hot driveway, she stepped into the shade of the orchard while Josh got something from his car. She settled herself against the trunk of a peach tree, knowing that every wet part of her would instantly be caked with dust.

He joined her with a Walkman radio and two sets of headphones. "Any good stations around here?"

"Of course." Picking at the tree bark, she told him the best rock and country stations, only adding the classical station as a feigned afterthought. A black ant crawled across her hand and she shook it off.

Josh fidgeted with the dial, his face at first perplexed; he settled against the same tree, sitting so close their shoulders almost touched. Then he placed headphones over her ears. Something by Mozart washed through Emily like a cooling river.

She chewed her lip. A magnetic current was shimmering between them. Just like with Scott. She closed her eyes and tried to ignore it, tried to lose herself in the music.

"Emily." Joshua's voice startled her, dead serious all of a sudden and right in the middle of a phrase.

She blinked. "What?"

"I have something to tell you."

Me too! she thought, panicking.

"I kind of thought — well, I —" Joshua's brown finger traced a treble clef in the dirt. "Well, uh, I'm coming to the university in Fresno."

"In *Fresno? Why?*" But she didn't need to ask. Fresno was just a half hour's drive away.

And Joshua's eyes told her his choice had nothing to do with the local scenery, nor the qualifications of the professors.

"Oh Josh —" Her eyes blurred and she jumped up. The motion jerked the head-phones out of place. With fumbling fingers she removed the headset. But then Joshua was there, patiently readjusting the tiny speakers for her. It almost seemed comical, the two of them linked by the same Walkman. But it wasn't funny at all. She turned away.

Her feet wanted to take her to the ditch, the place she went anytime she needed to think. A tug at the headset sent a deep blush pumping into her cheeks, for the black cord stretched between them like a leash, and Josh was following. He caught up quickly and walked beside her, not speaking. Beyond the music in her ears — something more modern now — she could hear the lazy hum of insects, the assertive rush of water through the weir. It was still going south, toward San Diego.

"So that wasn't the best news in the world." Joshua's voice sounded pained through the music.

Words and feelings tumbled like socks in a dryer, and suddenly she was reduced to babbling. "It's just — well, I don't want you to shortchange yourself. Music courses are better in LA or Long Beach — or San Diego."

"This Scott guy. You're still together?" Josh sounded deliberately calm.

"I didn't know how —" All that came out was a whisper. "I tried to call you —"

He shrugged. "I knew. You mentioned him in your letters. I just didn't mention him back."

Emily sniffled, wiped tears away. She reached out to him. "Josh, I — really, I — it's just — oh, *I* don't know!" Then she turned

away because the current between them was
dancing wickedly.

His hands settled on her shoulders.
"Don't cry, Emily." He sounded miserable.

She leaned against him, but the sun was
beating down so fiercely that even the
slightest contact was uncomfortable. "It's not
your fault, Josh."

Joshua took a deep breath. "Are you and
this guy — uh —" He shuddered. "God, what
am I saying? It's none of my business. You
must hate me."

"No!" she cried, shaken. "I could never
hate you." She faltered. "That other thing.
The answer is no."

Joshua gave a long sigh. Both of his arms
wrapped around her waist. The announcer
announced one of Bach's English Suites; crisp
piano counterpoint spilled into her, making
her fingers twitch, trying to catch some of the
notes. By now Scott would've been kissing
her . . .

She blinked the tears away and bent over
to peer into the ditch. On the sandy bottom,
flecks of iron pyrite — fool's gold — glinted in
the sunlight. Bumping against Joshua, she
squatted down among the foxtails and other
weeds growing at the water's edge. Her bare

toes felt gritty. "I used to play here all the time when I was little," she said in a gulpy voice.

Without a word he knelt beside her as she pointed out the pyrite, the polliwogs. The spiderlike water skaters; the water weed that floated on the surface like four-leafed clovers. In the distance came the rumble of a freight train pulling a load of refrigerator cars.

"Well, would it be — okay — if I was around?" Josh asked.

She blinked again and looked at him, really looked. In his warm eyes pain was mixed with a lot more. Quickly he turned to face the vineyard fronting the opposite ditch bank.

"I —" A coppery dragonfly buzzed into her face. She jerked away, toppled sideways. Joshua's hand shot out; she grabbed for it, but gravity claimed her and she slithered shoulder-first into the ditch. A second splash announced Joshua's abrupt descent. Cool mud swirled around them. "The Walkman!" she cried. In the confusion of arms and legs and the soft slippery bodies of terrified polliwogs, she groped for the radio.

"Got it," said Joshua. "Lucky — didn't even get wet."

Once again dripping, Emily stood up. "I'm *sorry!* This stupid dragonfly flew right at my face, I —"

But Joshua grinned up at her. "I think we've just found the coolest place in town. Quite awesome, actually." And he extended his hand.

"Are you serious?" she cried. But knowing Josh, he was. She giggled. "This is crazy!" she said, slipping back down to sit beside him. "This is totally, absolutely positively crazy!"

"And you love it, right?" His fingers intertwined with hers, almost casually, but it certainly didn't feel casual.

Her own fingers explored this new way of linking, flexing, curling, into the pockets between his larger ones. Their arms pressed together; her heart began thudding unevenly. She could feel what was coming, on hold ever since last summer . . .

Joshua's free hand carefully set the Walkman on the ditch bank behind them. "Is *this* crazy?" he murmured, bending toward her with Bach sounding in their ears. At last, he kissed her.

The breath drained out of her.

"Is it?" he persisted.

Dizzily she reached out to him, and there he was, holding her in a slippery, muddy embrace. Only the mud didn't matter. "No," she whispered.

"I wanted to do this last summer." His voice was faint.

"I know." The shadowy memories of music camp were no longer vague and elusive. Joshua playing his sax. Joshua taking the boys in his cabin on a sunrise hike. "You'll be a counsellor again this year?" Suddenly she needed to know so desperately it was a physical pain inside her and the waiting interminable.

"God yes! Aren't you?"

Mutely she nodded, dazed by the warmth in his eyes, by the envelope of sunlight caressing them, by the fact that Joshua had actually kissed her and was about to do it again.

A voice in the back of her mind nagged momentarily. *How on earth are you going to explain to Scott?* He wouldn't exactly be thrilled.

But Josh was kissing her. No room for Scott. Somehow the shadowy memories, the wistful daydreams, had solidified into 3-D living colour. This Joshua was more than memories, or words on paper.

And much more than a shadow.

# ONE WASTED SATURDAY

It was Saturday.

The wind had been screeching like a mad cat when Kevin awakened in the morning. Now snow was blasting across the prairie in white clouds that made him wonder if there really was a world out there.

Not that it mattered.

The blizzard would be doing him a favour if it blew the world away. Or if it blew him away instead, in a swirling white haze.

But there was no chance of that. He sat buckled onto the front seat of his uncle's old Nissan wagon, staring down at legs that couldn't feel anything and would never walk again. His wheelchair was folded up behind his seat, his cat Neptune perched on top of it, yowling in distress at the motion of the car. And his cousin Todd was driving, leaning forward to see the road.

Kevin's stomach lurched as the wind plastered more snow across the windshield.

He still got nervous in cars. After a year spent in hospital and then rehab, from the front seat the hugeness and motion of the outside world sometimes left him feeling like a raw egg without a shell. Times like this, none of the new skills he'd learned seemed to amount to anything. They couldn't take away the crazy fear. And they sure as heck couldn't put him on skates again. Not ever.

And now Dad was on his way to Toronto for a meeting, so here he was stuck going to the farm for a week.

"We should've stayed in town." Todd peered at the space where the road was supposed to be. "The folks would've understood."

Kevin grunted. He'd never had much use for Todd. They didn't have a thing in common. And these days Todd had a way of making him feel like a little kid being babysat. That really sucked, coming from his slightly younger cousin.

Something like a dark hole appeared in the blowing snow. A green road sign leapt out at them: Milestone 1 km.

"Almost there," Todd sighed.

*Don't you think I know it?* Kevin felt like yelling. *I've been going to your stupid farm all my life.* But he kept his mouth shut. It didn't feel like they were getting anywhere. And that suited him just fine.

A pair of headlights poked through the whiteness; a car whooshed past and was gone. The broken yellow line vanished, then reappeared at a cockeyed angle. Kevin's hands went clammy inside his mitts. He wasn't ready for this.

Why couldn't he have stayed home? He could've managed on his own for a week. Sure, it would've been hard — and probably lonely — but anything was better than being patronized. A sudden pressure on his shoulder startled him as Neptune's black furry body brushed against his cheek. Kevin reached for the cat and settled the warm animal on his numb lap. It probably looked wimpy, bringing his cat along, but he'd never gotten around to asking the neighbours to help out.

The town of Milestone swept by. Mostly it was a false lull in the storm, a suggestion of dark shapes that were really the grain elevators. Better that, than to be able to see clearly. There were too many places like this, small towns with their arenas, where he'd come as just one of the guys on the team. These days he was a one-man team, and there sure as hell wasn't anybody cheering for him. At least, not anybody that mattered.

"It's not far now." Todd cut into his thoughts. "But we still could end up in a ditch."

*Of course we could end up in a ditch. Anybody could, you dumb yo-yo.* Maybe Todd wasn't patronizing him, just revealing his own stupidity. Todd the clod. Anyone who'd spent even one winter on the prairies had seen empty vehicles littering the roadsides like soft drink cans after a major storm. So what else was new to talk about? How many emergency candles were packed in the box of supplies on the back seat? What brand of matches Aunt Marion had put in?

Behind them came the hum of a motor. An instant later a Ford half-ton truck was beside the wagon, then pulling ahead, leaving behind a dense cloud of snow that enveloped them, obscuring all traces of the road. In spite of himself, Kevin gasped.

Todd made an impatient sound and cranked down the window, thrusting his head out. Kevin shivered. Neptune hissed at the blast of cold air and sprang away, probably leaving a grid of scratches on his legs, but Kevin couldn't feel a thing. He realized he was clutching the arm rest as if it were a bed rail, just the way he'd done so many times in hospital, when he was so mad he'd wanted to crush the world into pulverized nothingness. Or when he'd tried to pull his unresponsive body into a more comfortable position. He forced his fingers to let go.

The road reappeared, a faint grey blur. Kevin sagged with relief.

Todd squirted a jet of windshield antifreeze and the wipers swished out a clear watery patch. "I can sure as heck think of other things to be doing right now," he muttered.

Hot anger raced up Kevin's neck. "I never asked to come to your farm. If I had my way, I'd still be home."

Todd looked embarrassed; he clicked on the radio, catching a Roto-Rooter commercial in full swing. "I didn't mean it like that. I've got this impossible algebra assignment, and we've got a major essay due in English next week."

"Well don't worry," Kevin said sourly. "I'll keep out of your way." Between his own homework, Game Boy and the TV, maybe it wouldn't be so different from home. There wasn't much you could do stuck in a chair.

He checked his watch. Three-fifteen. What a waste of a perfectly good Saturday. Well, it could've been good. Last year.

Kevin shook himself and shut his eyes. On the radio, Mick Jagger and the Stones were wailing out "Satisfaction", a real improvement over Todd's limp conversation. Maybe the last part of the trip wouldn't be such a bore.

"— dangerous highway conditions with low visibility and blowing snow." The announcer's voice jolted him. "The RCMP have closed all roads leaving the city. I repeat, all motorists are advised to refrain from travel until further notice."

"Now they tell us," Todd said with a shaky laugh. And then his voice went sharp. *"Jesus!* Is that guy ever coming up fast!"

Kevin twisted around. A pair of headlights and silver truck grille were bearing down on them. A moment later there was a solid roaring wall beside them as the semi pulled out to pass. Kevin's heart slammed against his chest like a hard shot into the net.

"Bastard! You'll run me off the road!" Already Todd had the window down and his head out.

The windshield wipers were useless in the maelstrom that followed. There was whiteness everywhere. Zero visibility. Kevin sucked in a terrified breath. His mouth was dry.

"Kev!" Todd yelled. "Steady the wheel for me!"

Nausea rocked him. No. He couldn't. Memories exploded all around.

"Damn it, Kev, help me out, will ya?"

His hands were ice. He could smell sweat, probably his own. But now the wheel was beneath his fingers, just like . . . In his mind he heard it the way he'd heard it a million times before, Jessica's terrified squawk, then her moan — "Oh God, oh my *God!*" as the tires skimmed over ice, as the concrete bridge support hurtled toward them . . .

Todd's head was back in. "Whew! Thanks!"

Kevin just sat there. Once again there was grey road ahead of them. But the yellow line was in the wrong place. Pale headlights stared at them. A blaring horn . . .

A yell wrenched its way from his throat. There was a violent swerve. They veered into whiteness. With a solid *whump* the car jarred to a complete stop.

Stunned silence, that wasn't quiet. Blood pounding in his ears. There was a funny whimpering sound that seemed to be coming from himself. And the radio was still on.

Todd swore and slammed both fists on the wheel. Then he turned. "Kev . . . are you okay?"

With a great effort Kevin pulled out of it. Managed to laugh. "Yeah, I've had this happen before." They were stuck. In a ditch. It was nothing major. Not with survival gear in the back seat and a full tank of gas.

"I hope the other guy's okay," Todd said weakly. "If he's hurt, it's my fault. I better go check."

"It's your neck, not mine," Kevin muttered. Let Todd play hero if he wanted. There was absolutely nothing he himself could do. Especially with his heart still jumping like a scared rookie, and his throat and eyes burning from all the memories.

Frigid air flooded the car as Todd got out. Kevin turned up the heat full blast, then watched over his shoulder while his cousin's dark shape melted into the storm. Loneliness ripped through him. He'd managed not to think about Jessica for awhile. But it still hurt. And these days he was useless; would girls ever look at him again?

A purring Neptune padded into his lap, obviously pleased that the car had stopped. Kevin rubbed his eyes and stroked the cat's sleek black fur.

Todd was back. More snow swirled in. "I'm walking back to Milestone," he gasped. "There's a woman and baby in that car. She's passed out over the wheel, and the baby's screaming and won't quit." He gave Kevin an odd, measuring look. "Will you be okay, Kev?"

"Of course I'm okay. Go." Kevin waved his cousin away. But he couldn't quite seem to catch his breath. Once Todd had gone, he realized Neptune was gone too. The stupid cat must've darted out while his cousin stood there talking. Kevin turned off the radio; he didn't really want to hear about low low furniture prices. He yelled out obscenities that he'd rarely used before the crash. Then, except for his breathing, except for motor sounds, all was quiet. The car rocked in the buffeting wind while snow scratched eerily against the roof and windows.

How long would he have to wait? And what about Neptune? Hopefully the cat would've slunk under the car for cover instead of taking off across a wheatfield. With a wind chill of 2300, he wouldn't stand a chance if he set out for home. *It wasn't fair!* For a terrible black instant Kevin wished he were dead.

He shook himself. Opened the door and called for Neptune. The wind snatched his voice away. All he could see was snow with yellow wheat stubble poking through.

What about the people in the other car? Were they hurt? Todd hadn't said if the engine was still running. If it wasn't, and the woman didn't come around, they'd both be in bad shape. That baby was even more helpless than he was.

Kevin jerked the door shut. Heat was escaping. And there was no way he could make it to that other car. His wheelchair would get stuck in the snow. In fact, ten to one he wouldn't even be able to get it out of the car.

Jessica. Once he'd started, it seemed he couldn't stop thinking about her. The way she'd touch his hand, then tilt her head and laugh. Her hair, dark and straight; the way it would fall over her shoulders, especially when she wore that pink sweater; the way it felt when he touched it . . . He choked out her name, then rubbed his face. Jess, who'd always made him feel good. Just driving around with her that day, a hockey game that night . . . Jess driving, nobody's fault, really, except maybe she'd been going a little too fast, but nobody could've predicted that icy patch . . .

Kevin swore. Wiped his eyes, leaned back. That was a year ago. It was over. Jess was dead.

He was here. Now. Stuck. In a bad spot. Just like the people in that other car.

Would it be long before help came? There'd been plenty of traffic. Probably a pickup would come by soon. The RCMP would be patrolling. He could flag someone down.

Nothing came except for the wind and more snow.

What about Todd? Kevin shuddered and adjusted the heater vents. The side windows were fogged up. Had his cousin been blown away from the highway? A blizzard could fool you, covering road surfaces until everything looked the same. Todd might be lost in some-body's wheatfield. In a wind chill of 2300. And those people in that other car would be get-ting awfully cold.

It was stupid to let his idiot legs keep him trapped like a baby.

Kevin fumbled for the back seat, feeling for the box of emergency supplies and mentally thanking his aunt and uncle for put-ting it there. Flares. Thermos of coffee. Tins of soup, can opener, Primus stove. Candles. Raisins, nuts. Cups, spoons. Matches. Blankets and sleeping bags were on the seat.

He unbuckled his seatbelt. Grabbing the back of the seat, he twisted himself around. Could he boost himself over?

The thought left him breathless. With several heaves he forced the wheelchair over behind the driver's seat. He sucked in a deep breath, braced his hands on the back of the seat, pushed hard. No luck. "Oh come *on!*" he grunted, hating his dead lower half. He twisted and strained. No luck. Then he saw it, the safety grip just above the door. He grabbed it, pulling and pushing at the same time. All the weight lifting he'd done in physio had paid off. Centimetre by centimetre he hoisted himself up. For a long, awkward moment he dangled. His heavy legs were pulling him down. In a desperate lunge he grabbed his wheelchair. He was over.

He felt as winded as if he'd just played a hard scrimmage on the ice. But a strange sense of elation skipped through him. From this angle everything looked different. It took a lot of pushing and shoving and smashed fingers, but at last it worked. His chair sat there in the storm, waiting.

Panting, Kevin checked the supplies beside him. What was most important? He squeezed his eyes shut, now forcing himself to remember the accident. Cold. He'd been cold, so terribly cold. The woman might be in shock. She and the baby could be headed for hypothermia. They'd need blankets.

Kevin made the transfer into his wheelchair, dragging blankets with him. He was losing strength. *Would* he be able to help? And then he had to laugh with relief. Neptune's snow-covered body scampered back into the car.

"You fur-brained turkey!" he gasped. But this was no time to sit there talking to a cat.

He strained to turn his chair. The small front wheels kept getting stuck in the drifting snow, and it took all his strength just to move. The wind flung snow into his eyes, but he needed both hands to keep his balance, to keep the chair moving. For an instant he saw the yellow centre line through low sheets of blowing snow. Almost halfway there. The red tail lights of the other vehicle drew him like a magnet. The wind was making so much noise he couldn't tell if the engine was running or not. In spite of the cold, sweat dribbled down his back. It was a long time since his body'd had to work so hard.

He'd made it. Trembling with exhaustion, he tugged at the door of the other car. Just as Todd had said, a woman was slumped over the wheel. The thin wail of a baby reached his ears, but from his position Kevin couldn't see it. Awkwardly he draped a blanket over the mother, then twisted to look for the kid. Where was it? The back seat?

He gritted his teeth and tried to position his chair so he could open the back door. But the snow was too deep for maneuvering. He'd have to roll back in his own tracks and try another approach. Why couldn't he *walk*, damn it?

Angrily he forced the thought from his mind. Straining, he backed onto the highway. The buffeting wind was going against him, a raw force that kept trying to roll him like a tumbleweed. Panting hard, he set his brakes. A few minutes' rest would help. Where the hell was Todd?

He tensed. Cutting through the wind was a sound that sent panic screaming along his nerves. The drone of an engine! The last thing a driver would expect to see in a blizzard was a wheelchair parked in the middle of the highway. Why hadn't he thought to set off the flares?

Over his shoulder he saw headlights. Coming fast. His hands fumbled like wet dishrags as he released the brakes and grabbed the wheels.

There was a sickening squeal of brakes. Tires grinding on snow. Any second now he'd feel the impact . . .

One final crunch of tires. A motor rumbling. Engine heat. But no impact. Kevin turned and saw a bumper maybe a metre away. Doors slammed.

"What the —?"

"— matter with you? Almost hit —"

He couldn't talk. He tried to gesture toward the car, but his body was jelly, jelly that wanted to ooze right out of his chair and onto the road. He couldn't hold himself up any longer. Brown splotches swayed before his eyes, roaring in his ears . . .

"Kevin. *Kev!*"

Todd's screaming voice, far away. Something shaking him. Cold wetness on his face.

His eyes blinked open. Todd was bending over him, jacket unzipped, looking scared right out of his skull. A second vehicle, an RCMP cruiser, was parked in the middle of the highway. Flares glowed pink. The blizzard kept on whipping snow around as if none of it mattered.

"Kev, are you all right?"

He was groggy. He couldn't think.

"Is he hurt?" A sharp voice nearby. There was a burst of static on the police radio.

"I swear, I never hit him!"

Kevin struggled to lift his head. "I'm okay," he gasped. "In the car — the people?"

"They'll be fine," said an officer.

"Kev, what the hell were you *doing?*" Todd's voice trembled. His face was blotchy and pink from the cold and exposure; a glossy bead of frostbite whitened the tip of his nose.

"The baby," Kevin stammered. "I got worried. I got blankets."

Todd's eyes widened. "Good show, cousin!" And he grinned.

"Damn stupid fool thing to do, if you ask me." "— dangerous." Other voices muttered. Kevin looked up at several pairs of legs.

Todd extended his hands. "Want to get going? This guy has a chain, and said he'd give us a tow."

The words warmed something inside Kevin. For some reason he no longer felt like a kid being babysat. "Great." He thought maybe he managed a smile.

"Need some help?" He heard an anxious query as Todd gripped his upper arms.

"Nah, we've got this one down to a T." Todd made it sound as if he picked Kevin up off the highway every day.

Kevin almost laughed. He hadn't known Todd had it in him. "Yeah," he agreed. Meeting his cousin's eyes and grasping his elbows, he began the count. "One . . . two . . . *three!*" He lifted his weight as Todd heaved, and then swivelled around so that he was back in his chair.

The bystanders were still murmuring. The blizzard still raged.

"Man, you had me *scared!*" Todd said as he pushed Kevin back across the highway.

Kevin still felt dazed. He found himself blinking with the flashing lights. Red. Blue. Even the headlights were flashing on the cruiser, catching individual snowflakes as they whipped by.

"Yeah," he said at last. "I know the feeling. I had *me* scared, too."

And then he laughed. "Hey, look." There, watching from the driver's seat, was a round black face with two pointed ears. "If that stupid cat hadn't escaped . . ."

So he hadn't come zooming in like Lindros or Gretzky. But somehow, things had changed. He shook his head. Amazing. He'd actually gotten himself all that way across that snow-covered highway in a wind chill of 2300; he'd draped a blanket over an unconscious woman . . .

"Hey Todd?"

"Yeah?" His cousin pushed him alongside the Nissan, and Kevin realized he'd have to sit in the back seat the rest of the way. There was no way they'd be able to get the chair safely down the incline of the ditch.

"You froze your nose." He wiggled the wheelchair arm, yanked it out so he could reach to open the car door. "And . . . I know you're pretty busy — but if you get sick of studying, I'll have you an arm wrestling match sometime."

Todd's eyes narrowed.

Kevin squirmed in his chair. His cousin was no idiot; he couldn't've possibly missed picking up on a certain attitude problem.

"Okay," Todd said slowly. "Yeah, I think I can find the time."

# SARAH AND ALEXANDRA

They say having a car makes a girl sexy.

Sarah wasn't so sure about that. But things had certainly changed since Alexandra came into her life.

Sarah and Alexandra. It wasn't quite the way it sounded. Sarah's parents weren't concerned in the least. In fact, they'd introduced the two of them and encouraged the relationship.

Alexandra was the older of the two, twenty-four to Sarah's seventeen. Already Sarah felt she'd learned a tremendous amount.

Alexandra was a 1968 Volkswagen Beetle, and Sarah loved her dearly. She knew all of Alexandra's habits on the road; she knew every little dent or scratch, every rust spot. Alexandra was the most beautiful car in the world.

"The *d* is crooked."

Sarah jumped at the critical voice by her elbow. The leg of the *r* began to trickle, a forest-green enamel streak following the pull of gravity along Alexandra's pale blue flank. Sarah sucked in a sharp breath, held it, and with a tiny square of her old nightgown she caught the errant paint and blotted it before any damage was done.

Then she looked up at Jaime. "Don't scare me like that!"

Her best friend shrugged, tossing brown hair back over her shoulders. "I thought you heard me coming. I was talking to you."

Sarah bit her lip and looked at the green paint splotches on her hands. The brush was dripping onto the driveway. Now the concrete would forever bear evidence of Alexandra's formal naming ceremony. If Jaime hadn't shown up she'd be finishing right now. Freehand painting wasn't all that easy. Once you stepped away from it, it was hard to get the next letter lined up right. "I was concentrating," she said.

"Obviously." A trace of sarcasm nagged in her friend's voice. "If I can tear you away from your car long enough, I've got some news."

Sarah looked longingly at the *Alexandr* painted two thirds of the way down Alexandra's right passenger door. It did a good job of camouflaging the long scratch. The *d was* a bit crooked, but she'd never admit it to Jaime.

"Hang on just a sec while I paint the *a*," she said. "Then I can listen better."

Jaime muttered something that wasn't terribly ladylike and scuffed her runners on the warm concrete.

Sarah gulped in another long breath and held it. Her knuckles were white as she clutched the tiny brush. She dipped it into the small can of paint, shaped the wet hairs into a clean point, and trembling, touched it to Alexandra's side. Right away she knew the angle of the *a* was off. But it was too late. Well, it was Jaime's fault, for distracting her. But then, you couldn't expect to be perfect. Not all the time.

"Done," she said a moment later. She put the brush to soak, scrubbed most of the blotches off her hands, and looked up at Jaime. "So what's new?"

"You're as bad as a guy," Jaime muttered, and leaned against Alexandra's right front fender. "When you got that car I thought we'd have instant transportation and instant fun. Instead, what do I get? *No* transportation and *less* fun because you're always doing something to that old thing."

Sarah compressed her lips, trying to keep the hurt inside. Maybe she *hadn't* paid as much attention to Jaime lately, but . . . She lifted the left windshield wiper to remove a poplar leaf. "I'll get used to her after a while," she said lamely. She knew it wasn't true.

"Oh sure. You've had that car almost all summer. We're running out of time."

Sarah met her friend's eyes, then looked away. The summer *had* sort of slipped by, lost in the glow of owning Alexandra. She knew she'd never forget this magical time. It was like . . . well, it was like pride mixed together with hardly daring to believe that she could be so lucky. As she got to know every square centimetre of Alexandra she marvelled and made plans. It gave her a sense of purpose. A feeling of control.

"Then let's go someplace," she said to Jaime. "As soon as the paint dries. What did you want to tell me?"

Jaime groaned and pounded Alexandra. "There you go again! How long will *that* be, five hours?"

Sarah glanced at the fender to make sure Jaime hadn't dented it. She knew it wasn't likely, but . . . "Maybe half an hour," she lied. "If we stay in town nothing'll hurt it much." Actually the thought of dirt and insect flecks sticking in the paint made her cringe, but she had to at least *try* to make Jaime happy.

"Well that's more like it." Jaime's face brightened. "You'll never guess what I just found out! Dustin got a job!"

"Oh," Sarah said carefully. Jaime was forever swooning over Dustin Finlayson, and you'd think a job would mean that he was out of circulation. "What's he doing?"

"He's working as a car hop at B & G's! Let's go, and maybe he'll wait on us!"

A car hop? It seemed like a wimpy sort of thing to do. But then, it couldn't be any worse than what Michael Stanley was doing. *His* job was to stand on the street corner dressed in a gorilla outfit, advertising vacuum cleaners. Something inside her softened as she thought of Chris. This summer he was working in a garden supplies shop; her mother had seen him there each time she'd gone in for bedding plants. Now that Sarah had Alexandra, she'd been offering to pick up the next bag of fertilizer or whatever, but Mom was pretty well stocked up.

Sarah ran her thumb and fingertips along Alexandra's antenna. "Okay. Maybe we could stop by at Henderson's afterwards. I overheard Mom saying something to Dad about needing another hose."

Jaime's eyes glinted. "Oh, sure!"

Sarah looked away. "Well, it can't hurt to look." She pulled a square of rag from her jeans pocket. There was a bird splotch on Alexandra's roof. As she scrubbed at it, she felt laughter welling up to join Jaime's.

"Sure," Jaime said again. "And then you'll be looking at wheelbarrows and watering cans and weed spray . . . "

Sarah squatted to look at the paint job. *Alexandra,* it said in neat dark green lettering. It wasn't so big people would yell out when she drove past. She sniffed the clean paint smell and longed to touch it, but didn't dare. *Be dry,* she willed. She blew on it gently, then opened the door for Jaime. "Come on," she said. "Get in."

*"Well!"* Jaime gave her a regal smile. "Now *that's* service."

It was heaven to slip behind the wheel, engulfed in a capsule of warm air. Alexandra's steering wheel was like condensed sunshine beneath Sarah's fingertips. She turned the key in the ignition. With a loud buzzing sputter, Alexandra faithfully came to life. Sarah let out a blissful sigh. With a firm push that dipped and curved, she shifted Alexandra into reverse and they backed down the driveway.

Jaime cranked down her window and set the wing window so that air circulated pleasantly throughout Alexandra's interior. "This is the life," she murmured, resting her head against the back of the seat as they turned onto Salteaux Avenue. "What more do we need than a couple of gorgeous men?"

Sarah peered anxiously into the rearview mirror. A white pickup was following too closely. She lifted her foot off the accelerator. Alexandra obligingly slowed down, puttering along at a sedate speed. The impatient driver swerved into the left lane and zoomed ahead.

"Why didn't you gun it?" Jaime said. A critical look flickered in her eyes.

Sarah glanced at her friend. "Alexandra doesn't have as many cylinders. Besides, have you noticed the price of gas lately?"

With a languid motion, Jaime dangled her arm out the window. "As I was saying, all we need now is a couple of gorgeous men . . . "

"What about Dustin?"

"I doubt we can convince him to come away with us."

Sarah spotted a familiar gawky figure hurrying along the sidewalk. If she wasn't mistaken, it was Tim Giesbrecht from A Band at school. He might only be going into grade ten, but he did play a mean trombone. "There's one," she said. "Shall we stop?"

*"Him?"* Jaime laughed contemptuously. "I mean a *real MAN.*"

But Alexandra wanted to have her say. Sarah's hand settled on the horn, and Alexandra's nasal *beep-beep* called out to Tim as they drove past. Sarah waved. Tim waved back, after a first very stunned look flashed across his face.

"See?" Sarah said as she settled back into the driver's seat. "A woman with a car has power."

Jaime's nose crinkled. *"Any* woman could have power over that one."

The sun shone all about them; a whole medley of vehicles shared the street in a vibrant dance. A red light stopped them. There, on the opposite corner, was Michael Stanley in his black gorilla outfit. Sarah found herself wondering if he got hot, dressed like that. Alexandra wanted to beep, so Sarah allowed her to.

The light went green. Sarah's foot hit the accelerator. Alexandra might be low on cylinders, but she was pretty quick stepping away from a changed light. With a pleased little gurgle, Alexandra shot forward, for a minute surprising a lazy black Z28 in the next lane. Alexandra *beep-beeped* with pride, and the gorilla/Michael waved. When they drove past a group of demonstrators carrying "Save the CBC" banners, Alexandra BEEP–be-beep-beeped so wildly that some of the demonstrators waved back.

"*Sarah!*" Jaime's green eyes were narrower than usual. "What's got into you?"

Sarah shrugged, trying to repress a grin. It had something to do with Alexandra. But Jaime'd never understand, so she said nothing.

Jaime leaned forward and tried to turn on the radio.

"It doesn't work," Sarah reminded her. "I'm buying her an AM/FM/cassette player when I've saved enough. I just got another pet-sitting job, and Mrs. Kumar wants me to babysit Friday."

"Oh," Jaime said, looking straight ahead. "How come you always refer to it as *she?* It's only a car. You'd think you were in love with it or something."

Sarah swallowed the hurt and tapped her fingers against Alexandra's steering wheel. Maybe Jaime would understand when she got her first car. *Possibly.* Sometimes her imagination seemed somewhat limited.

They swept onto the bridge, with its soft-coloured stone carved figures. A long line of wheelchairs was rolling along the bridge sidewalk. Some of the people in them were carrying signs. Sarah craned her neck. "We need adequate public transportation too," one of the signs said. Alexandra *beep-beep-beeped* in support. Sarah agreed, although Jaime's chin was looking rather stiff.

B & G's, at last! For some reason it had seemed like a rather long ride. As they approached, Jaime's face lost its jawbreaker look and reverted to its normal appearance.

Sarah held her breath and cautiously eased Alexandra over the speed bumps. One. Two. Made it! Sarah parked in the stall closest to the large plate glass window.

"There he is!" Jaime cried, waving. Then she actually pouted. The closest order button was on Sarah's side of the car. "Get me a large rootbeer float," she said.

It didn't sound like such a bad idea. Sarah ordered two. If her passenger were in a better mood she might've tried ordering a litre of 10W30 oil for Alexandra too, as a joke, but she suspected it wouldn't go over too well just now.

Dustin brought their floats. The mugs were nicely frosted over.

"Oh, he's the absolute *best,*" Jaime said with a sigh.

Best *what,* Sarah was tempted to ask. It always seemed to her that Dustin had that macho over-confident look about him. Chris, on the other hand, had a thin thoughtful face and soulful brown eyes.

"Two rootbeer floats? Roll up your window just a bit, please." Then Dustin went to the trouble of looking inside the car. "Sarah! When'd you get the wheels?"

Sarah longed to be able to blend in with the fabric of Alexandra's seat covers. She did shrink backwards a bit as Jaime leaned across her and said brightly, "Dustin! I didn't know you worked here!"

"Yeah. I got the job last week." Dustin set the window tray in place. "That'll be $4.33, please, including tax."

Jaime managed a charming scowl. "What a ripoff."

"Yeah. Everything's a ripoff these days." Dustin lounged around, actually leaning against Alexandra as Sarah fumbled for money in her wallet. She'd have to remind Jaime to pay her back later. "So, Sarah," he continued, "you busy burning up the streets these days?"

"Not really . . . " Sarah began.

But Jaime had already said it for her. "Not really. She's so in love with her precious car that she's afraid to drive it in case somebody breathes on it."

There was more hurt to swallow. Sarah did, dutifully, as Dustin punched out the change from his money belt.

He slapped it down on the tray. "Here's your receipt." His fingers accidentally brushed Sarah's. They were cold, probably from handling the rootbeer floats. "Well, you can burn on down this way any time you feel like it. I'll keep them from coughing all over your baby. You can always count on D.F., you know, the Dustin Factor." Whistling, he sauntered away.

"What a ripoff!" This time Jaime's scowl was not at all charming.

Sarah looked straight ahead at the grille of an immaculately groomed '57 Chev. She swallowed a sip of her float. "I didn't say a thing to him."

"You didn't have to," Jaime said scornfully. "He was so impressed by your *car.*"

Sarah carefully wiped her mouth with the serviette. "I can't help it. It was your idea to come, remember?"

Jaime slashed at the mound of foam and ice cream floating in her drink.

They didn't stay very long. When Sarah pressed the pickup button, a different car hop waited on them. She was glad. Jaime didn't seem to care one way or the other.

Even Alexandra was feeling rather down as she pulled out. She forgot all about the very worst speed bump in the whole parking lot.

"Thanks," Jaime muttered as she lurched forward. "I really needed that."

*Well you asked for it,* Sarah thought. Her fingertips curved around the steering wheel as she waited for a chance to pull out into traffic. She halfway didn't feel like stopping at Henderson's anymore, but then, fair was fair. She wouldn't say anything for the time being, though. Jaime'd come around once she had the chance to simmer down.

Jaime lifted her hair off her shoulders. "The D.F. is just an immature twit anyhow. A mere child." But her face looked stiff again as they headed back down Salteaux Avenue in the other direction.

The wheelchairs were gone from the bridge, but the CBC Protection League was still out in force. Even so, Alexandra just gave a little *beep-beep*. She wasn't much in the mood. There was Michael the Commercial Gorilla waving from his street corner. All he got was a small *beep*. The gorilla waved back, but it might have been because it was just his job.

"That *child,*" Jaime said loftily, "can stand out there in the rain with his rootbeer until he washes down a storm drain, for all I care."

Sarah thought it unwise to remind her friend that it hadn't rained in two weeks and wasn't likely to start doing so, just at the moment. In the block ahead two kids with bicycles were waiting patiently at the crosswalk for a chance to get across the stream of heavy traffic. Her foot hit the brake, not too hard. The taxi behind her was not amused. It swerved around her as she stopped, and the next car in the left lane had to do some spectacular brake work when its driver realized that two children were crossing the street.

"I want to stop at Henderson's," Sarah said, once she thought it was safe.

"Fine." Jaime seemed unconcerned. Her right hand dangled out the window.

Tim Giesbrecht was still hurrying along Salteaux Avenue, this time on the opposite side of the street. Sarah glanced at her friend. "Shall we give him a lift?"

"Does your mom approve of picking up strays?"

It was too late. Alexandra *beep-beeped,* though, as they sailed past. Tim's skinny stooped shoulders jerked in surprise; then he saw them and waved.

Sarah waved back.

Jaime simply looked airily out the window, her head lifted proudly as the Queen's.

Henderson's was blissfully cool inside and smelled of fertilizer and potting soil.

Chris was helping set up a display of planter boxes. Sarah saw him right away, a lean compact figure in T-shirt and faded jeans. Her feet kept trying to pull her over in that direction, but she dutifully went to the next aisle to check out the prices on the hoses. For some reason the numbers had a funny way of slipping out of her memory.

"Well look who's here! I didn't know you worked here, Christopher." Sarah spun around at the sound of Jaime's sweet voice.

Chris looked over his shoulder. His arm muscles bulged as he hefted one end of a planter box. "Oh, hi, Jaime." Half a second later his attention was back on his work.

"*Well!*" Jaime sniffed as she sauntered over to Sarah and the hoses. "I don't believe there's a single male on earth who knows the first thing about manners."

The corners of Sarah's mouth were twitching. She quickly turned toward the sprinklers. The next time she looked, Chris was gone.

"This is boring," Jaime sighed a few minutes later. "Let's go."

Chris still hadn't reappeared. Sarah gave one last hopeful look at the Employees Only door in back, and stepped outside into the heat. She'd check Alexandra's paint job here in the parking lot, and then once they got home, she'd check the oil. She hadn't looked at it since yesterday morning.

And then she saw Chris. He was sitting in a red three-quarter-ton truck, trying to back a flatbed trailer full of planter boxes over to the service door.

Sarah bit her lip. The parking lot looked kind of small and crowded for that kind of maneuvering. At least Chris would get a glimpse of Alexandra. If she timed it just right and got in after he'd backed the trailer to where it was supposed to be . . .

The trailer obviously had a mind of its own. It was behaving exactly like Graham Starky, whom she'd babysat far too many times. It seemed no matter how hard Chris tried to line it up with the door, the minute he shifted into reverse, the thing would veer off to the side.

"Can't he even drive?" Jaime said derisively.

Sarah glanced quickly at Chris' face, just once. He didn't look too happy, so she pretended to examine some potted yellow potentillas.

*THWUNKKK!*

Uh oh. Chris would be embarrassed about hitting something. Casually, very carefully,

Sarah looked over her shoulder. A strangled yelp caught in her throat.

That Graham Starky of a trailer was leaning heavily into Alexandra's left front fender and driver's door. No, it was doing more than leaning. Alexandra had already crumpled in defeat.

For an instant Sarah just stood there. She felt sick. In dazed slow motion she went over to inspect the damage.

"Is that your car?" Chris asked. His soulful brown eyes looked like the eyes of a kid who'd just been caught shoplifting, and his face was an interesting shade of geranium.

Sarah nodded. She was sure she'd cry if she tried to speak.

Alexandra's door was grimacing in pain. In one spot the paint had been scraped off, revealing her naked skin.

Chris swore vigorously. "I'm *sorry*," he said. "I'll go get the manager." With rapid steps he headed toward the service entrance.

"Where'd *you* learn to drive, turkey?" Jaime yelled after him.

Sarah's chin wobbled. She looked at her car and then at her friend.

"Jerks," Jaime muttered. "They're all jerks. Useless." She surprised Sarah by tracing her finger along the dent. "What a ripoff.

Good thing it wasn't the other side, eh? At least your paint job's okay."

Sarah sniffled. Jaime gave her a little hug.

The manager appeared, a stubby sort of man with an efficient-looking clipboard. "Oh boy," he said. "That one hurt. We're terribly sorry; this never should've happened. But don't worry, young lady. We'll take care of the whole works." He bent closer to inspect the damage. "Looks like it's just the door and the fender; any body shop should be able to fix that."

He babbled on and on with polite reassurances about their insurance coverage, until Sarah was ready to gag. Meanwhile Chris did not reappear and Jaime's right foot was tapping restlessly. When everything was finally settled, more or less, the last person Sarah expected to see was Tim Giesbrecht.

Obviously Henderson's was on the way to wherever he was going. He wandered onto the parking lot, shoulders still stooped, but his face was twisted with dismay. "Sarah! What happened to your car?"

Jaime was rolling her eyes and muttering under her breath.

But Sarah looked up at Tim's concerned eyes. "Chris Hastings backed into it." The words came out like jagged pieces of glass.

She wished she could make her chin quit wobbling. If Chris would at least show his face she'd feel like he was actually sorry. But no, he didn't have the nerve, and Alexandra needed major repairs, and . . . She turned away and quickly wiped her eyes.

Tim was shifting awkwardly from one foot to the other. "Oh geez, your car . . . I bet it feels like your leg got bashed in."

Actually it did, only worse. Sarah tried to smile. She ran her hand along Alexandra's pale blue roof. "At least it's not fatal," she said.

"Well, I'd better be going. I just thought — well, seeing your car banged up and all, I just thought I'd see if you guys were okay."

"Wait," Sarah said, as the tall lanky boy began shambling away. "You looked like you were in a hurry. Need a ride?"

Tim turned back. "Yeah, thanks! I was on my way to work — I sort of do sweeping and stuff at Burger King, you know — but I missed the bus. My boss'll kill me if I'm late."

Jaime was displaying an acutely pained expression.

Sarah turned her back on her friend. She grasped the handle and cautiously tugged at Alexandra's door. It didn't budge. "I guess we all have to get in the other side," she said. There was a huge lump in her throat that wouldn't go away. But after all, Alexandra was a car, not a person, and she could be fixed. She wasn't *really* in pain.

She slid behind the steering wheel. The driver's seat still felt the same, the gearshift steady beneath her hand. She flipped the passenger seat forward. Surprisingly, it was Jaime who flounced into the back seat.

Tim climbed in, his head nearly brushing the roof and his gangly legs taking up all the extra space on the passenger's side. "What year car is this?" he asked. "Geez, it must be older than any of us."

Sarah turned the key in the ignition. With her familiar sputter, Alexandra made it clear that she still meant business, smashed door or no. As she backed up, there was a faint scraping sound as the left tire brushed against the crumpled fender. But it only happened with the wheel turned sharply. Sarah shifted into first and waited in the driveway, right turn signal winking cheerfully as traffic rumbled past.

*Beep-beep!* Alexandra sang out as Chris stood in the main store entrance, watching. Slowly, he waved. Sarah waved back and pretended she didn't see the humiliated look on his face.

"Geez, I really appreciate the ride," Tim said as they pulled out into traffic. "I was sure I'd get fired, for sure."

A strange snorting sound came from the back seat. Sarah glanced in the rearview mirror. Jaime was faking an asthma attack.

Sarah relaxed. It felt good, melding into the flow of traffic. She checked the gas gauge. Once she'd dropped Tim off, she'd fill up and give the windows a good polish. And somehow she'd have to figure out what to say to Jaime. The more she thought about it, the more she realized why it was that Jaime was so cheesed off at her.

Alexandra's steady bumblebee engine chortled reassuringly.

And then one piston skipped a beat, only to resume at a quicker pace. The old car hurried ahead as fast as her driver's foot would allow. There in the left lane . . .

There in the left lane was a beige 1968 Volkswagen Beetle. He wore two forest-green peace symbols on his back, and as Sarah drew abreast of him, she saw the name *Dylan* neatly painted in red on his right rear fender.

Alexandra purred.

# SOMETHING ABOUT THAT GIRL

I don't know what it is about that girl. I mean, we've known each other over a year now. And it's about half a year since things started getting interesting between us. But sometimes she makes me so mad I'd give all my hockey cards to throw her in the lake. With her boots on.

Well, maybe not my Gretzky rookie card.

Right now I bet half the people in Kaslo are saying, *"There goes that crazy Lewis kid, looking for his girlfriend."* School got out a little while ago and if Karen doesn't smarten up we'll miss the bus and have to wait till six, when Minnie Frazer locks up the confectionery for the night. Minnie won't mind giving us a ride home, no problem about that. But I kind of thought if we sat together on the bus we could sort it all out.

Karen McConnachie is tiny — she barely comes up to my shoulder — and incredibly strong. She can be pretty funny sometimes when she's relaxed. The other side of the coin is, she's so shy sometimes you practically need jumper cables to get her to talk. And so sensitive that if you look at her wrong, she'll take off on you.

She's been avoiding me since third period. Geometry. I *did* look at her wrong today, and it didn't even have much to do with her. But she never gave me a chance to explain.

* * * *

I felt like an idiot racing along the sidewalk opening doors, looking for her. The credit union, the coffee shop. The antique store. The food co-op. The farm supplies place.

Everybody was staring at me, I just knew it. Loggers, waitresses, the food co-op lady. Even though we've been here over a year, we're still outsiders. Parts of the Interior are like that, where some families stick around for generations.

But that wasn't the only reason they'd be staring, no such luck. If the news wasn't out already, before long they'd be staring twice as hard, and quit talking the second I got within earshot. *Did* they know?

*"That's one of them Lewises, eh?" "Yeah. Not the bad one, he's gone."* Heads shake, faces get tight,

*maybe some guy lights up.* "*Good riddance, that one.*"

I winged a rock at a garbage can. It clunked and bounced into the street. Dad always says I let my imagination get carried away. Now I'm not so sure, not anymore.

I looked through the window of the Overwaitea store. No Karen. But people saw me looking. Probably they *did* know. All of a sudden it was hard to breathe.

"*So which one's this?*" "*Dunno – how many kids they got?*" "*This one's Stu . . . something like that.*" "*Stan, I think's his name. My kid's got a class with him at school.*" "*Who gives a – what he's called. Better keep an eye on him too. One rotten apple spoils the whole lot.*"

My face got hot, just imagining. That's the way it is, though, half the time. People watching me. Just waiting for me to make one bad move.

I ran some more.

A logging truck was coming down A Avenue, about to round the corner. I waited. Panting. And wondered what would happen if I decided to make a run for it, across the street.

Ward. He's like a bad smell that follows me everywhere. He got himself back to Calgary in a hurry after his grad, but he might as well still be here. With a brother like Ward, a guy's reputation's shot even before he gets a chance to prove himself. Guilty with no trial.

The ground shook beneath my feet. The air was disgusting with diesel exhaust, and for a bit, everything else was blanked out by that big truck. Motor rumbling. All those wheels churning beneath a load of logs, crunching gravel in the street, chains rattling, flaps flapping. Those trucks freak me, up close. Something hypnotic about the underside of the thing, the wheels — it's like they want to suck me right underneath. *Squish.* "*Oops. What was that?*" "*Only Stan Lewis, no big loss.*" Or the other scenario. A weak link in a chain. One quick snap, the load shifts, it dumps. Crushed by falling logs. Not a fun way to go.

I glanced at my watch and tried not to swear. Only five minutes till the buses left. Even if Karen happened to be waiting for me across the street at the gas station, we'd never make it, not now, not even if we sprinted like mad.

That girl! She's so touchy.

I wished I could tangle my hands in that wavy dogfood-coloured hair of hers. Gently, of course. Not like . . . I'd hold her and look at her, and she'd look at me, and I'd tell her a couple of things face to face. Because I didn't even do anything wrong. Not really. And then, I'd hug her.

It kept replaying itself like a bad dream.

* * * *

Sitting there in geometry. It's cool when teachers seat us in alphabetical order, because that usually means I end up sitting right in front of her. Half our classes are like that. It feels good just knowing she's there. She can never see over my head to the chalkboard, though, so sometimes I like to kid around, make her squirm a little.

Sitting there in geometry. Old Paterson's up there drawing chalk pictures and babbling about the special properties of right triangles. My mind's someplace else. It's drawing pictures too, and they're so ugly I want to puke.

Ward's in jail. He raped a girl in some parkade. He had his knife out.

I feel like screaming obscenities, except that's something *he'd* do. I feel like running over the tops of all the desks. Like kicking that stupid green chalkboard so hard it busts into a zillion pieces. Except I'd probably bust my foot instead and the whole class would wonder what the heck got into me.

I look down at my notebook and discover it's crumpling in my hands.

Karen pokes my back. "Stan!" she whispers.

She doesn't know. Probably she won't have a thing to do with me once she finds out.

Another poke. "Stanley! What's the matter?"

I can't face her. I go all stiff. My pencil snaps in two in my hands.

Old Paterson natters on and on at the chalkboard, but suddenly it's way too quiet in the desk behind me. Slowly I turn to check on her.

That Purina Dog Chow hair is down over her glasses. Her pencil is drawing straight hard lines across the top margin of her assignment.

Danger zone.

I try to make an idiot face so maybe she'll smile.

She doesn't. "How come you're ignoring me?" She whispers so soft I can hardly hear. She looks at her math book, not me.

I can't tell her. Especially not in the middle of geometry, for Chrissakes (oops). Maybe at lunch. *Maybe.* But why should she be so touchy? I'm the one whose guts are so twisted out of shape I want to puke all over my desk.

"Back off! Can't you even let a guy breathe?"

Damn! I never meant it to come out like that. My stupid mouth. Sometimes it blabs out any old thing, and not necessarily what I mean.

I can't see her eyes at all. But her chin looks like a rock with a bad case of the wobbles. I've had it. Maybe she'll talk to me in two days. If I'm lucky.

* * * *

The truck was gone, and I felt like I could breathe again.

Standing there on the corner, looking up and down the streets. Useless. I'd been running around like a geek, and now we were going to miss the bus anyhow. Kaslo's so small, with only eight hundred people, that if Karen had wanted me to find her, I would. I ran back to Front Street.

Down the hill, toward the lake, the same old scroungy black lab was nosing at a soft drink cup that somebody dropped. As I watched, an old green GMC half-ton drove by. The guy driving whistled. The dog loped along beside the truck for a while.

In back of me, I heard the sound of our bus shifting gears as it climbed uphill on its way out of town. I felt like saying something, but didn't. When I looked, it was crawling along the roadcut like an orange-yellow cater-pillar. A moment later it rounded the bend and was gone in the forest. So much for that.

Desolation.

I didn't fit in. Not here, not anywhere. I wasn't like the others — might as well have a big label CITY KID, or, GEEK, on all my clothes. With Ward gone, I'd almost thought I'd be able to make a place for myself.

Wrong. It was pretty clear I could go to Mars, and Ward would be there waiting for me.

And now I was running around all over town, looking for that stupid girl. As if it mattered.

I went into the Red & White. The door clanged.

Minnie Frazer looked at me with knowing eyes. "Hi, Stan. Miss the bus?" It wasn't the first time I'd come in asking for a ride.

"Yeah," I muttered, and tried not to look at her fat arms that made her old sweater balloon out like blue sausages. "Probably Karen did too." I went to the rack of chips and found myself a large bag of Cheezies. Once my gut untwisted, they'd help stave off the hunger pangs. I hadn't been able to handle lunch.

Minnie waited there by the cash register, the original blimp, probably almost sixty. Thinking like that, I was afraid to look her in the eye when I set the Cheezies down. And more to the point — had she heard about Ward yet? It wasn't exactly the kind of thing that'd be on the local news, but in places like Silver Ledge and Kaslo you didn't need a radio or TV. Word got around. Sometimes half the town knew what you were up to, even before you'd made up your own mind.

The register dinged and the drawer sprang open. "I saw Karen about five minutes ago," Minnie wheezed. She slapped my change onto the counter. "She was heading down toward the Moyie."

The Moyie. Actually, it kind of made sense. "Thanks, Minnie. See you at six." I pocketed my change and ripped the bag open on my way out.

I went on down the hill toward the lake. Even after a year living here, I still find myself stopping just to look. Kootenay Lake lies there like a giant finger over a hundred kms long, deeper than I like to think about. It's like it catches the sky, and the forested mountainsides that plunge down to meet it. The Purcell Mountains loom above the opposite shore, and right now they were glaring down on me like a whole row of judges. The peaks were already covered with snow. Halfway down the slopes the yellow tamarack looked like somebody'd spilled a lot of paint. When it got down here, we'd have to do some serious thinking about winter. Even now the air was cool and smelled of wood smoke.

It was so insanely beautiful. I wanted to cry like a lost kid. The world didn't have a right to be this way. Not when Ward kept screwing up.

I squeezed my eyes shut and chewed hard on a mouthful of Cheezies. I was losing it, I just knew it. But how many other guys end up with a big brother who's psycho? Who gets *mean,* and out of control. You want to have somebody to look up to, someone to stick up for you when things get scary. Instead, you get beat up. I swallowed. Blinked. Looked around again. Nothing had changed much.

The West Kootenay country's like that. Solemn, so beautiful sometimes you feel you don't deserve to be there looking at it. There's a kind of stillness. Almost . . . wisdom. It leaves you thinking those mountains must know one heck of a lot more than the stupid race called mankind. Or should I say *Homo sapiens,* to include both halves.

\* \* \* \*

So she's at the Moyie.

Back in the old days before the road was built, everything going in or out from the north end of Kootenay Lake had to go by stern-wheel paddleboat. That's the Moyie. It made all those trips.

It's docked on dry land now, down by the water, and it's a museum. It's not a bad place to go, if you feel like thinking about the past and seeing lots of old things.

But the hell I'm going to pay admission just so I can find that girl! Like hell.

I glance over that way, sort of casual like. No sign of that red-and-black checked China shirt she always wears.

I'm not so sure I want to see her, anyhow. She'll look at me with those hurt green-brown eyes behind her glasses. And then I'll feel like I have to apologize. I can't — I *can't*.

Oh God, I'm losing it. What a wuss. I just — *can't* — it's ripping me apart inside so bad. Sometimes I wonder, is it really worth it? Nobody understands. All those years at the receiving end. Ward Lewis's own private punching bag. But the minute he flips out in public, the whole world thinks I'm just the same.

*"You really gotta watch them Lewises."*
*"You're tellin' me? Hey Bob, you gonna let your*

*girl keep going out with that kid? She might come home hurt real bad one of these days."*

God, I'm doing it again. Fifteen years old, and bawling like a little kid.

I hear a chainsaw. A boat going into the marina in the cove. Big ugly noises coming out of me. I just can't quit.

Something cold and wet snuffles by my ear.

I yell.

It's only the dog, that old black lab. I grab him and hang on. He seems to understand; he washes the side of my face with smelly dog slobber. His fur is bristly and all dusty. I'll probably get a zillion flea bites. But it's kind of nice to have company.

After a while the dog gets bored and pulls away. I hear the scrackly sound of plastic.

My Cheezies!

I yell at the mutt and pelt him with a couple of rocks. He yelps and makes himself scarce. He made my Cheezies pretty scarce too.

So it's just me and the lake. Every now and then I hear the water slapping against the pebbles on the beach.

He raped that girl. Hurt her, *really* hurt her, in a way that probably won't ever go away. It sits there inside me like a giant clump of horse manure. Won't I *ever* be able to look people in the eye?

Something moves nearby. I try to freeze. Can't.

Now it's too quiet. Is it her?

"Stan . . . "

I go all rigid. But what the hell, she saw me cry once before. After that big fight when we were all stranded in the bush, after that accident last spring.

"Stan, what's the matter?" She sounds scared.

I can't begin to tell her. Heck, I can't even make myself look at her.

All of a sudden her arms wrap around me from behind. Her face presses against my shoulder. She doesn't say a thing.

So we sit there. Karen quiet. Me, gulping and snuffling like that mutt, trying to get it back together.

At last I swallow. I fill my hands with rocks from the beach. Stand up. Karen doesn't say anything. I throw the rocks, throw more, keep throwing until my stupid arm's limp by my side. And then I tell her, because there's nothing left to do. My voice is dead.

She reaches for my hands. Hers are warm, mine are freezing. She looks up at me. "Stan . . ."

Talking's not her forte. But I can see a whole lot in her eyes. They hurt. For me. She's about to cry. The wind ruffles her hair.

I reach for her. She presses against me, wraps her arms around me. She's strong, and it's almost like she's giving some of that to me. Her head's against my chest. She's crying too, I can feel the wetness through my shirt. My fingers tangle gently in her hair, I stroke her head, hold her close to me.

At last Karen finishes what she started. So what if it took her five minutes. "I just don't know what to say." She looks up at me. Her glasses are a mess. Her eyes still hurt. But I see something kind of like love there, too. Another logging truck goes through town. "I don't know *what* I'd do if it was me," she whispers.

"Thank God it's not." I stand there. Empty. A thousand years old.

But she's still here. A real live human being. Close to me, because she wants to be.

So who the heck is Stan Lewis?

Not the kid who can't handle his sick brother.

The other one, the one she sees.

# OF TIME AND TEETH

*Mrs. O'Keefe has lost her teef*
*And can't tell where to find them . . .*

Joan's feet clattered down the metal steps. The bus lurched away, belching the stench of diesel into the half-darkness.

Wind-swept drizzle found her cheeks and clung there, tiny atoms of coldness; the air smelled of low tide. The animal bellow of the fog horn shattered the wet dawn while traffic lights and street signs creaked, groaned, swayed, with each gust. In the distance bell buoys clanged in the heaving sea. Early spring on the island was sometimes no different from winter.

*Leave her alone and she will call JOAN*
*Who will be able to find them.*

Joan checked her watch. 6:47. She came on duty at seven.

Lurking behind the naked limbs of huge and solemn oaks, the Victorian hulk of Blenkinsop Manor awaited. Once a tea merchant's house, the nursing home wore an eerie, almost otherwordly aura so early in the morning. Wavering shadows flickered, flame-like, beneath the eaves, in the surrounding branches, like lingering memories of previous owners and departed patients.

Joan's friends all thought she was crazy to give up her Saturdays for the part-time job as nurse's aide. Joan herself never would've dreamt it possible, not until her Y-group did a service project and she'd met Mrs. O'Keefe. Then everything changed and she knew that someday she would be a nurse.

*Mrs. O'Keefe has lost her teef...*

The other aide, Gwyn, had made up the rhyme. Toothless, senile, and completely helpless after a stroke, Mrs. O'Keefe was the kind of patient who made a person shudder at the thought of growing old. But there was something about the look in the woman's round blue eyes — a perpetual question of some kind — that had tugged at Joan from the first time she'd sat there spooning soup into Mrs. O'Keefe's open mouth.

She hurried up the slippery back steps and was engulfed by prickling warmth and the twin odours of must and disinfectant. She hung up her jacket and locked away her purse, tiptoeing down the dimly lit corridors, for the old ladies were allowed to sleep until seven. Only the nursing station sat apart in a blaze of light. Joan clocked in, then stepped into the staff room for a quick cup of tea. Mrs. Blaylock, the head nurse whose word was law, seemed never to have discovered instant cocoa, or coffee.

The hall lights clicked on. Seven o'clock. Joan gulped the last of her tea and reported for duty as Gwyn rushed in, red-cheeked and disheveled. "Nasty morning out there!" Gwyn gasped.

"Is it ever." Joan could hear Mrs. Ellingham stirring. But first she looked toward another room which still lay in darkness. "How's Mrs. O'Keefe?" she whispered.

Gwyn smoothed her crooked collar, then smoothed the white front of her nurse's uniform.

It was beastly to be wrenched out of bed in the dark on a blustery morning. Sometimes she needed two hours to feel all in one piece. Times like this it was hard to face the tender-eyed girl who showed up regular as the tide every Saturday. No doubt in time she'd have her fill and leave, just like all the others.

"More confused," Gwyn replied, her eyes thoughtful. "She keeps calling for you." Then she grinned. "We really had a time of it this past week, let me tell you. For all her goings on, you'd figure somebody flushed her precious 'teef' down the john. Even Mrs. B. wouldn't do. Nope, it had to be 'my Joan'."

Joan smiled. Mrs. O'Keefe was forever missing her teeth, even if they were safely in her mouth. Yet somehow the forgetfulness didn't irritate Joan. In an odd way she associated the old woman with the grandmothers she'd never known.

It had started with an awful mistake. Gwyn, rushing to get all the patients up for breakfast, had forgotten Mrs. O'Keefe's dentures on the bedside table. "My teef! My teef!" the old woman wailed, until Joan came to the rescue. It was only her second day at work. She'd slipped the false teeth in, accidentally placing the upper plate on the lower gums, while her patient's eyes widened in astonishment. A muffled protest rose from Mrs. O'Keefe's throat and Joan realized, mortified, that she'd trapped the woman's tongue.

"You found my teef," Mrs. O'Keefe declared once Joan set it right. And from that day on she trusted Joan implicitly.

Joan couldn't understand it.

"Nurse?" Miss Aiken was calling. "May I have a bedpan?"

"Coming, love," Gwyn called.

Joan followed, stopping at Mrs. Ellingham's bedside. Mrs. Ellingham had all her wits about her; her only problem was that she was ninety-three and no longer able to care for herself, so her sons and daughters, in their sixties and seventies, had put her in a home.

"Good morning, Joanie," Mrs. Ellingham said. "Would you help me sit up, please?"

"Sure." Joan smiled. After Mrs. O'Keefe, she was fondest of Mrs. Ellingham. The first part of her morning routine was to loosen the ties that bound the elderly woman's hands and feet to the bedrails. As Joan's fingers went to work on the firm knots, she couldn't repress a stab of indignation. According to the night shift, Mrs. Ellingham was so strong-willed she refused to ask for help getting up to use the toilet. After a few dangerous falls the doctor had ordered her restrained for her own safety.

"All night I heard the wind tearing at the treetops," the proud, frail woman remarked as Joan adjusted the pillows. "A good day to work on the afghan, no doubt."

"You make such beautiful things," Joan said, her hands busy pulling underwear from a drawer. "I don't see how you do it."

She was constantly amazed at the colourful items which seemed to multiply as rapidly from Mrs. Ellingham's knitting needles as her own pet gerbils did in their cages at home.

The woman's face crinkled into a smile, but a trace of melancholy lurked in her faded brown eyes. "I have nothing but time, my dear." She flexed her bony fingers but did not mention the painful arthritis. "'Tis the price a body must pay for being so very old."

Joan smiled as she handed over the washbasin, the comb, the mirror. "There you go, Mrs. E." Miss Pankratz was next. Joan hated pulling away so quickly, but that was part of the job. Mrs. Blaylock scolded if the women weren't all up for breakfast at seven-thirty. Gwyn was already on her third patient.

"My teef! Joan! My Joan!" The wail echoed down the hall.

Joan reached for Miss Pankratz's denture cup and caught Gwyn's eye. "Should I?" She felt like dropping everything for Mrs. O'Keefe, but Mrs. Blaylock was very strict about staff allowing patients to become dependent on any one aide.

Gwyn shrugged. "Why not. The old girl's been calling for you all week, give her a break."

Joan met Mrs. Blaylock with her starched cap and demeanour halfway down the hall. "This will have to stop," the nurse said curtly. "She's disturbing the other patients. I must get her doctor to up the chlorpromazine."

Joan tightened her lips as she turned on the bedside lamp. She really wondered if the medication was part of Mrs. O'Keefe's problem; so much was said these days about old people being given too many prescriptions. "Good morning, Mrs. O'Keefe," she said, reaching for the trembling, bird-like hand.

*"Joan."* The white-haired woman gave a sigh and looked up at her with the trust of a small child.

"We'll turn her today while you're here." Mrs. Blaylock glanced at the chart at the foot of the bed. "She's been awfully cranky about who comes near her, and I'm afraid she may have bedsores."

Joan winced. The constant pressure of mattress and pillows against bony areas could wear right through the skin, if let go for too long. Bedsores were said to be very slow to heal.

"Mrs. O'Keefe," Mrs. Blaylock continued, in tones a teacher might use with an unruly small child. "You've been making far too much noise. You're disturbing the other ladies. Joan is only here on Saturdays, you know. You won't be allowed to see her at all if you keep this up."

The old woman's round blue eyes widened.

Joan tensed. Without looking at the nurse, she produced a damp facecloth and began wiping Mrs. O'Keefe's tissue-paper skin.

"I'll be dead tomorra."

The soft dry voice rattled Joan so badly that the facecloth slipped down among the pillows and sheets. She tried, not very successfully, to keep her voice steady. "You'll be here to see the roses bloom, Mrs. O'Keefe."

"I'll be dead tomorra."

"They get like this when their minds go," Mrs. Blaylock said in a low voice. "Don't let it worry you, dear." And she swept away to answer the telephone.

Joan's hands shook as she put the false teeth in. They were still shaking as she combed the old woman's thin white hair, and the comb found a snarl.

"Oh!" Mrs. O'Keefe exclaimed, reaching for her scalp.

"I'm sorry!" Joan stammered. She took a deep breath and put the comb away. "Ready for breakfast, Mrs. O'Keefe?"

The trusting eyes never wavered from her face.

On to Mrs. Hicks, to Miss Marie Larchmont who insisted on being called by her first name, and then Mrs. DiMaggio. Joan was jittery. No one had died during her brief tenure at Blenkinsop Manor. Certainly old people were bound to pass away. Both of her grandmothers had died before she was born, so it hardly seemed a loss. But if she came to work next Saturday and found a stranger in Mrs. O'Keefe's bed — well, it would be awful.

She bumped against Miss Pankratz's wheelchair as she went by with Miss Aiken's breakfast tray. The tea slopped over in a brown puddle. She dropped one of Mrs. Southey's half-slices of toast, butter-side down.

"Is something wrong, Joanie?" Mrs. Ellingham asked, competently sprinkling white sugar onto her porridge.

Gwyn grinned. "I bet she's thinking about a certain young man. Those teenagers have one-track minds." It was fun to tease the kid once in a while. She took everything so seriously. Besides, it helped lighten the mood. It never hurt the old girls to laugh a little. The staff either, as far as that went. Agnes Blaylock could sure use a good dose of humour. That nurse seemed more married to the job than to the husband she mentioned vaguely every now and then — if he was even still around.

Joan blushed. "All I did last night was watch TV."

"And watch the late late LATE show . . . "

Actually, she'd been in bed by eleven — not that it mattered. Mrs. Ellingham's faded eyes held a wry twinkle.

"My granddaughter has asked me to dinner," she announced. "She'll be here to fetch me at eleven." In a deft motion she peered at her slender wrist watch, then shook her head. "My eyes aren't so good anymore. Joanie, what is the time?"

It was only eight fifteen.

At eight forty-five Joan helped Mrs. Blaylock turn Mrs. O'Keefe so the old woman lay on her side. She stayed to massage lotion into the ancient skin, wishing she could ease away the red wrinkle marks. Then she picked up the dainty music box that sat on Mrs. O'Keefe's bedside table. It was a jewellery box, she supposed, though it had nothing inside; a delicate old curio with the look of hand-painted china, dust-pink roses traced with gold. She carefully wound the key and "Tea for Two" tinkled out. Mrs. O'Keefe smiled in her childlike way and hummed tunelessly. The music box seemed to give her immense pleasure.

Joan tiptoed away.

Miss Marie Larchmont needed help getting up with her walker. Then Mrs. Ellingham got in a dither because her skein of green yarn rolled beneath the bed. Joan retrieved it and looked sadly at Mrs. Southey. The old woman sat staring out at the grey morning. She insisted young girls in gingham frocks were skipping rope just outside the window, and was chanting along,

> *Solomon Grundy, born on a Monday,*
> *Christened on Tuesday,*
> *Married on Wednesday . . .*

Only the rose garden was out there, at the moment little more than a damp patch of thorny skeletons. Joan closed her eyes and ears to the mumbling and tried to imagine the warm, heady scent of roses in full bloom. And wondered if Mrs. O'Keefe would ever smell them again.

"Nurse?" Miss Pankratz called from her wheelchair. "Would you possibly have the time to read to me from my *Holy Bible*? I would so dearly love to hear a few Psalms again."

So Joan did that too, squinting at the fine print and stumbling over the strange hyphenated words. She looked up once, wondering how Mrs. O'Keefe was doing, but a stern look from Mrs. Blaylock reminded her that she was on duty for all the old ladies, not just one.

At ten fifteen Joan washed the floors. The area around Miss Aiken's bed was sticky with strawberry jam. At ten thirty Mrs. O'Keefe began calling. Joan went to her.

"Joan," Mrs. O'Keefe sighed, and reached for her hand. And as long as Joan sat there, the old woman lay quietly.

But Mrs. Ellingham needed to get ready for her outing, and Gwyn was helping Mrs. Southey in the tub.

"Joan!" The haunting cry echoed down the hall.

Joan winced. She gathered Mrs. Ellingham's horrible bandage-pink support hose and stodgy brown shoes from the closet and wished Mrs. O'Keefe would stop.

"She's a long way down the road, that one," Mrs. Ellingham observed in her crusty voice. "You must treat her well."

Joan flushed at the praise. "I try to do a good job," she murmured, looking at her white shoes. "I want to be a nurse."

Mrs. Ellingham nodded. "You'll make a fine nurse, Joanie." She gazed out the window, where bare treetops were flailing against the swollen grey sky. "It's a foul morning, it is. An old woman like me could catch her death." She sighed. "Might be a blessing."

"How —"

Mrs. Ellingham cut her short with a gnarled hand on the girl's supple arm. "You have everything to live for, Joanie. It's not so at my age, dear. I'm lonely, my Hiram gone twenty-six years now, and our own children beginning to go . . . "

"Nooo! My Joan! My teef!"

*Mrs. O'Keefe has lost her teef*
*And can't tell where to find them . . .*

Joan's eyes stung. Gwyn's silly rhyme was no longer funny.

Was Mrs. Blaylock trying to force a tranquilizer down the old woman's throat? Stupid pills! Or was it a needle? She wondered if Mrs. Blaylock had watched the recent TV feature on drugs and the elderly.

Rain-scented air swept into the nursing home, bringing with it the hiss of tires on wet pavement. Joan helped Mrs. Ellingham ease her skinny arms into a bulky wool sweater and then, again, into her heavy black coat. Her fingers hurried with the gaudy old-fashioned buttons. A stout dimpled woman in her forties waited.

"All set," Mrs. Ellingham announced. She wobbled as she leaned forward onto her cane.

The granddaughter took her arm but shot Joan a beseeching look. "Could you come with us to the car? I'm afraid —"

Mrs. Ellingham snorted. "They're all afraid. Afraid the legs will give way. Afraid of an old lady like me. I could make it perfectly well on my own, given the time."

Joan patted her stooped shoulder. "Can't have you slipping, Mrs. E. Doctor might say no more outings, and you know how much you'd hate that."

Gwyn stuck her head out the front door just as Joan and the granddaughter began helping Mrs. Ellingham work her way down the wet wheelchair ramp. "Now you be a good girl, Mrs. E," she called. "I don't want to hear you were chasing all the men."

The granddaughter looked decidedly shocked. Joan bit down to repress a grin. When the old woman glanced her direction, right eye closed in a wink, she sputtered with laughter. She just couldn't help it.

Gwyn watched from the doorway. The kid was good for the old girls, no question about it. But she wondered when reality would hit, wondered if she ought to sit her down and warn her about the grind, how it could go on and on for years on end, the lifting and bed-pans, the dotty minds. The grim ordeal of night shift, with the snores and the smells. And the silence.

"Nooo! My Joan! My teef!"

"Oh hush, Mrs. O'Keefe," Gwyn said. And she went to rub Miss Aiken's back. The poor old dear was so stiff she could barely move, but never complained, not a word . . .

*Buried on Sunday,*
*That was the end of Solomon Grundy . . .*

All the following week at school Joan tried to forget Mrs. O'Keefe's prophecy. But the old woman was forever beckoning, during French, during history. Joan was tempted to phone and ask if she was all right, but a morbid fear held her back. Maybe she should quit her job. It *would* be nice to have her Saturdays free.

In her mind she composed a thousand excuses. Mrs. Blaylock would likely go all stiff and huffy. The nurse was forever complaining how good help was hard to find. And Mrs. O'Keefe — she was senile, after all. A silly old woman. She would forget. *If* she was still alive . . .

Joan considered calling in sick when the alarm jolted her at five forty-five the following Saturday. Mrs. Blaylock would be hopping mad, but how could she face an empty bed? Or a stranger?

But could she leave Mrs. O'Keefe waiting with her trusting child eyes, waiting for her teeth, waiting to hum happily along with her treasured music box?

It was a still, silent morning as the grey dawn spread itself across the island. Crocus and daffodil silhouettes cheered the small plot beside the employees' entrance, yet a keen sense of finality emanated from the nursing home as Joan stood outside in the dark. She could still make a run for it. Pretend she had a sore throat, didn't want to infect the old ladies . . .

But what about Mrs. Ellingham? Sweet Miss Pankratz?

"This is Mrs. Davies," Mrs. Blaylock said as she introduced Joan to the overweight woman in *her* bed, in Mrs. O'Keefe's bed. "She's been with us for a few . . . "

Suddenly Joan wasn't hearing too well. The world shimmered, far away.

Mrs. Blaylock pulled her aside. "Mrs. O'Keefe died quietly in her sleep last Saturday," she said kindly. "Just before I went off duty that night, she insisted you get one of her things. Her family agreed."

"Her teef!" Gwyn said with a wicked grin.

Joan nearly punched her in the mouth.

Her hands shook violently as she unwrapped the tissue paper; she nearly dropped the parcel. She wished she could set it down and cry. But Mrs. O'Keefe's childlike smile was lingering in the room, in the air about them, registering her every move. Joan's eyes blurred; she blinked fast and most of the tears went no further than her lashes. She blinked harder at the cool ceramic touch of the music box in the cup of her hands. Gently she lifted the lid. Inside was a crisp slip of paper that said *Lydia O'Keefe* in black ink strokes.

Somehow she'd never thought of the old woman as someone who'd had a first name, or even a normal life, once. But there were plenty of other things she'd not thought about, either. Like a twisting kaleidoscope, images flashed, tumbled, tiny bits of translucent colour, then quietly rearranged themselves.

Briefly she held the music box against her cheek, then locked it away with her purse. It might be a while before she wound it, but there was plenty of time. She'd keep it on the dresser top with her other precious things. It was like a gift from a grandmother, something she could pass on to a daughter, if she had one someday.

Joan took a deep breath. She blinked again. Then she walked down the hall, head up, and at peace. "Good morning, Mrs. Ellingham," she said.

# RED TIDE

It was hot. Heat waves shimmered above the stretch of pale sand along the water's edge; the Southern California sun draped its heavy embrace across Erica's shoulders.

Something was wrong with the ocean.

Erica shook herself, blinked, and looked again. Earlier, from the motel room, she'd thought maybe it was the smog, or perhaps the sun playing tricks on her eyes, that made the water look so brassy. She'd even put it down to her mood, the end-of-holiday blahs.

But this was no illusion. From where she stood at the edge of the beach parking lot, it was very clear. The Pacific Ocean spread its vast reach to the horizon, not blue, but an odd murky colour. Up close, it was reddish-brown.

Erica turned to her sister. "It looks . . . *poisonous,*" she said, tugging at the strap of her swimsuit. There was a sense of her internal gravity letting go; her insides tried to settle but couldn't seem to find quite the right spots.

"Ewwwww. It kinda looks like blood." Ronnie's sunburned nose crinkled. "Think there was an oil spill or something?"

Erica shook her head. A group of kids pushed past, blasters spitting out rap. "There'd be cleanup crews," she said.

"There's people *swimming*. You won't catch *me* going in there." Ronnie shaded her eyes to scan the beach. "See Clark anywhere? He said he'd be here today for sure."

Erica shrugged. "I'm sure he'll find us, if you don't find him first." That was the worst thing about holidays, having to hang around with her sister. And now, Clark.

Clark Goodman was strange. He had the golden-bronzed looks of the surfer crowd, but his personality was pure nerd. He came from someplace she'd never heard of, and happened to be staying in the next motel room. It was funny, though — they rarely heard his voice through the wall, and never the TV. Clark was too polite. He didn't eat in the coffee shop. And though he loved the beach, he rarely went in the water, but seemed to prefer poking around looking at things.

Ronnie adored him. Their parents trusted him. Whenever Erica felt like bugging her sister, all she had to do was call Clark a diseased gerbil. Or an alien. That got Ronnie, every time.

"Let's go find some *other* guys to talk to," Erica said, kicking off her runners and worming her toes into the burning sand. "It's our last day, and Clark's about as thrilling as reading the phone book."

Hurt swam in Ronnie's eyes. "I don't know what you've got against him. He's the hunkiest guy we've ever known, and he's not the least bit snobby."

"Maybe he's HIV-positive — can't afford to be picky." Erica's foot shot upward, sending sand flying about in a satisfying spray. She wished she knew, herself, why she didn't like Clark.

She darted away from Ronnie's angry retort, dodging between occupied blankets and towels, avoiding kids and sand castles, crushed pop cans and cigarette butts, dog messes and broken glass. There was even the occasional flash of white shell, and tangled seaweed strands abandoned at high tide. She halted at the water's edge and stared with a kind of fascinated horror.

Small brown-stained waves rolled in asthmatically to fizzle against the firm sand. What had happened to the raw, churning power of the Pacific? This wasn't much better than Katepwa in a storm.

Erica lifted her hair off her shoulders and tentatively immersed her toes. The water was milky-warm, unlike the cool briny freshness which usually greeted her. Weird, very weird. But her skin was not eaten away by some caustic chemical; nor were the hundreds of waders up and down the beach in any kind of distress. The screaming, wheeling sea gulls overhead were acting like it was any old day — maybe they were colour-blind. Step by step Erica waded out until she stood hip-deep among swells which pressed past her toward the shore.

Two younger girls were standing nearby. One had a pair of binoculars. Erica got their attention and asked, "What's wrong with the water?"

The one with the binoculars giggled. "Gross, isn't it."

The other gave her friend an impatient look. "It's the red tide," she explained in a know-it-all voice. "Microscopic something-or-others. You know, from the signs?"

At that, Erica recalled the many posted warnings about the dangers of eating the shellfish during summer months. She glanced nervously at her legs — and yes, her hands were wet too. Could the stuff soak through skin?

The first girl caught her eye. "That your boyfriend?" she asked, nodding her head in a shoreward direction. "He's been watching you."

Erica's heart did a frightened lurch — probably some creep wanted to pick up a stray female. When she finally checked over her shoulder, she saw that it was only Clark. "He's just a friend," she said.

The girl gave her an envious look. "Send him my way if you don't want him."

"My sister's already first in line." Erica grinned and splashed over to Clark.

"Where's Ronnie?" she asked. With Clark you had to take the initiative if you didn't want to endure long silences. Behind her, wavelets broke impotently and dribbled back into the rust-coloured wash.

Clark's mouth smiled, but his eyes remained a steady impenetrable grey. They were almost too large and had a kind of intensity which never seemed to spill over into his personality. "Over there." He indicated a familiar pink-and-green towel.

Ronnie lounged about, sunglasses on and her Walkman headphones planted firmly in place. She shot Erica a towel from the bag. "Don't get any of that stuff on me," she warned, her voice too loud above the music which must be rattling inside her head. "We forgot to sunscreen," she went on. "I asked Clark if he'd do my back, but he said you'd better do it."

Erica hid her smirk behind the towel. It was all she could do to keep from rolling on the sand, laughing. So the gorgeous Clark Goodman had a thing about not touching girls' backs. She'd known it all along; the guy was useless.

"Scoot over." She sat down on the warm towel; sand clung to her legs and feet. Her sister's freckled back was sweaty as she massaged the perfumed cream into it. Looking out over the water, she had the oddest feeling that somehow this was no longer her home planet, but some alien seascape light-years away. "How can microscopic junk do that to the water?" she wondered aloud.

Clark sat down too, leaning back on his elbows. His bare feet extended well beyond the edge of his towel. "It's a massive population explosion of dinoflagellates," he explained. "This variety gives off a biochemical luminescence." Light glinted through his sun-bleached hair; it caught in the red stone of the single earring he always wore.

Maddeningly, Erica wondered why his looks weren't doing things to her. Maybe it was because he was such a nerd. Or maybe because of Tyler, back home? She smeared sunscreen onto her own shoulders. One of these days Clark would have to learn that it just didn't rate, going around talking like a textbook.

Ronnie giggled. "Clark, you sound like a scientist."

"I am one," he said in all seriousness, flicking grains of sand off his towel. "I'm a biochemist. I came here to —" He broke off and scanned the horizon, but all Erica could see out there was a boat.

She slapped at a sandfly which kept lighting upon her ankles. *Get real,* she wanted to say. But maybe Clark was one of those prodigies, and he took samples and stuff when they weren't around. In that case, this red tide would be a gold mine.

Ronnie's elbow nudged her ribs. *"Look!"* she whispered.

Erica followed her sister's gesturing thumb. As usual, Clark was the object, but there was nothing new about him, not that she could see. But just for an instant, the red glow in his earring seemed to waver. A prickly feeling skittered across Erica's scalp. She shook herself. Probably a wisp of cloud had passed in front of the sun. She stood up. "I'm going back to the motel."

"What?" Ronnie lifted the headphones off her ears. Her elbow grazed Clark's tanned arm and Clark, oddly, jerked away.

"I'm going," Erica said flatly. "With these waves, you can't even bodysurf. The waterslide's better than *this.*"

Ronnie pouted. "We just got here. And it's our last day."

A heavy, glum feeling washed over Erica. She almost wished their flight had been scheduled for today. That way they'd be up in a 727 heading for Calgary, looking down at clouds and mountaintops. None of this red water stuff. And Clark Goodman would be little more than a memory.

Clark chose that moment to ask if they wanted to go to Laguna Beach after supper. "Once it's dark, the water will be lit up like nothing you've ever seen before," he promised.

Ronnie was thrilled.

Erica wasn't so sure.

* * * *

His driving was abysmal.

It was dusk. All around, city lights were coming on, incandescent floodlights and flashing neon. It seemed to Erica that some parts of Los Angeles never got truly dark at night. Maybe that was the general idea; it would be pretty creepy being among millions of strangers in total darkness.

Clark's old Honda jerked with every change of gears. Erica was tempted to ask if she could drive. She'd done better with the half-ton, out on the farm, when she was thirteen. But it wouldn't have been polite. Besides, she was in the back seat. With a German Shepherd for company.

She had no idea where the dog had come from. Ronnie had asked right away, but Clark's reply had been vague, implying the dog just decided to come along for the ride. You didn't *do* that, pick up strange dogs.

In the front seat Ronnie was fidgeting with the radio. One minute mariachi music filled the car, all Spanish voices and guitars; the next it was the news. An instant later M.C. Hammer belted out. Ronnie hopefully leaned closer to Clark.

At the moment Clark was cowering in the on-ramp to the freeway. A lit-up truck roared by, an intimidating wall.

A wet slurp startled Erica's clenched fist. She looked over to the loving gaze and alert pointed ears of the German Shepherd. They were safely on the freeway now, though all around them traffic zoomed by at breakneck speeds. Erica sighed and put her arm around the dog. "Thanks, bud," she murmured. Something inside her wanted to laugh hysterically. She was having better luck with the dog than her sister was with Clark Goodman.

In front of her, Clark's neck was very straight and stiff. As Erica stared, the earring gave off a single pulse. She tensed. Back at the motel, they'd talked about that earring. According to Ronnie, it had flickered several times on the beach. But her sister'd been such an absolute dweeb. *"Maybe it's got batteries,"* she'd insisted. *"You know, like Mr. Toews' light-up tie?"* Erica checked to make sure she had her flashlight. If it was all a setup for a rape or something, well, you couldn't say she hadn't warned Ronnie. At least she'd taken that women's self-defence course. If Clark tried anything, he might just end up hurting.

At Laguna there was a fishy stench in the air. But Clark had been right. The sky was darker, and a pale white glow shimmered in the water. The breakers were long ghostly streamers combing the sand.

*"Awesome!"* Ronnie breathed.

Erica shed her runners. The sand was cool; she squiggled her toes and let the grains sift between them. Beneath her feet the beach recoiled faintly as a large wave exploded nearby. Erica ran toward it and waded in the rushing foamy mixture of sand and water, a fine salty spray dancing all about, a region where land and sea and air all met in an ongoing conversation.

"Come this way," Clark said, heading further south and away from the main beach.

Reluctantly Erica followed, turning on her flashlight. There was sure to be the usual stuff lying about which could be wicked on bare feet.

"Slow down!" Ronnie called. "I can't keep up!"

Erica dawdled, casting the flashlight in a wide arc. Every now and then the dog paused to mark new territory.

"What does he think we are, marathon runners?" Ronnie grumbled.

"Don't ask me." Erica clambered over rocks, some of which tilted as she passed. Her flashlight caught Clark perched atop a boulder. She found a spot of her own and turned off the light. Before her the ocean shone as if moonlit, but the moon wasn't up. "It's beautiful," she murmured. And she shot a genuine smile in Clark's direction, though she wasn't sure if he'd see it in the darkness.

She heard Ronnie sit down; she heard the dog padding about, snuffling at the odd, fishy smells. And so she sat there, gazing out over the water. There was a boundless energy in the ongoing march of the waves. Break . . . retreat . . . break . . . retreat, always the surge of restless water. Beyond it, the air seemed to vibrate in a way that she couldn't quite hear. She listened, straining, but could not identify the disturbance.

Without warning, the glimmering ocean sucked away from the shoreline with a deep groaning hiss.

"Aaaack!" Ronnie squawked. "What's happening?"

Erica leaped to her feet. She'd read about something like this once or twice, and it could only mean . . . "Tidal wave!" she yelled, and began scrambling toward higher ground.

*"Wait!"* Ronnie cried in a panic. "Wait for me!"

"Don't be frightened. My people are harvesting. You will not be harmed." Clark's voice didn't sound quite right. Something about it twisted Erica's stomach into cold pretzels.

"Ow!" Ronnie cried out. "I stepped on something."

Erica swore under her breath and shone her flashlight on her sister. Blood oozed from a gash in Ronnie's bare foot. A broken beer bottle glinted among the rocks nearby.

Ronnie hopped about, clutching her foot in one hand. "You and your weird ideas!" she wailed. She teetered and grabbed Clark's arm for support.

A strange sound came from Clark, a kind of terrified moan. The hairs on the back of Erica's neck quivered. The pale orb of her flashlight caught the image of blood smeared on Clark's arm.

The earring gave off frenzied blips and all the while, the water still hadn't come back to shore, and the dog was growling by her side.

Ronnie screamed, screamed again. She didn't seem to be able to stop.

Erica looked first at her sister and then back at Clark. His features were oddly transparent. He made a croaking noise and thrust the car key into her outstretched hand. And then he . . . wilted, or maybe he simply melted. His clothes fell into a heap. From them emerged a strange membraney thing which vaguely resembled a huge jellyfish. Only this one had a red blinking light, and two large grey eyes that stared up at her.

She wanted to do as her sister was doing, scream and run, but something held her. Her heart pounded in her ears as she stared at the creature. "You *are* an alien," she whispered.

The thing didn't answer. But suddenly a series of pictures crowded her mind. A whole community of translucent beings, all tinted in delicate shades of green and blue. They were shaped like nothing she'd seen before, mushy-looking cylindrical creatures with six or seven tentacle-like extensions on either end. All had large eyes at their midpoint, some grey, some violet. Only one had a red spot, and it was smaller than the others. Images of a silvery building . . . no, it could *move* . . . a craft of some sort? Creatures within, seeking . . . seeking what? Blue ocean turning rusty; seawater drawn up into the silver thing and then released, blue once again. The smaller creature, impatient, wanting to see what lay beyond . . . nameless shapes whirring before her; then the image of Clark Goodman.

Feeling faint, Erica sank down on a rock. The German Shepherd leaned against her in an affectionate manner as she gazed at what had once been Clark.

*"Erica!"* Ronnie's voice shrilled from a distance. "Get away from it!"

Yet she wasn't frightened. "The harvest," she murmured to the creature. "You came to harvest the — the . . . dino —" She stumbled over the long word. "And you wanted to explore, so they . . . gave you a human shape." She almost touched the thing to see if it really was as soft and glisteny as it looked, but at that moment another chunk of information slid into place. "But you weren't supposed to let anybody touch you." No wonder Clark had always shied away from Ronnie's impulsive, friendly gestures. Tenderness filled her as she looked at this fellow living being, which had always rubbed her the wrong way in its counterfeit form.

As she watched, the red light dimmed and went out. "No!" she cried. Tears sprang to her eyes. She wanted to help "Clark" but didn't have the faintest idea what "he" needed.

Vaguely, she was aware of sirens screaming, of lights flashing, seemingly from all sides. With a deafening roar the ocean came surging back. Waves slapped wildly against the rocks. There was a kind of shuddering in the air. At her feet the dog whined.

She looked again at the creature. Its grey eyes were clouding to flat chalky pits. "No!" She pressed her hand to her mouth, trying to stifle the sound, for now other people were tramping across the beach with high-intensity torches.

A blinding shaft of violet light spurted from somewhere, touching upon the alien. Erica shielded her eyes and cowered face-down among the rocks. There was a sudden change in the air pressure. Her ears hurt. Something in the air was pulling . . . straining . . . There was an intense painful crackling inside her ears, inside her head; she moaned in agony. Whatever it was burst free, and there was a sensation of something shredding the sky overhead. Then her ears popped. It was almost quiet. The age-old rhythm of the waves had resumed; the air was cool and felt like night.

Cautiously Erica opened her eyes. The rocks lay empty before her. An aching sadness clotted her throat. As if it understood, the dog snuffled in her ear and gave her a sloppy kiss. Beyond, the ocean was dark.

"Hey you!" a man's voice called. Suddenly a flashlight shone full in her face, and she blinked. "Seen anything funny around here? There's been a UFO sighting."

Erica shook her head. "No," she said slowly. "I was just out walking my dog."

Clutching the car key tightly in her cold hand, she went to find her sister.

# TRUCE

Winter 1967. The Summer of Love had come and gone. In San Francisco kids my age with long hair and freaky clothes were turning on and dropping out, preaching love and peace. I wanted to think I was one of them. But the fact was, I was stuck in small-town central California, miles and miles from where it was happening. Our school was still in the 1950s, while the rest of the world approached 1970. The other fact was Jim Holland. He was one of *them*. Except, he lived in Sierra Vista now.

I glanced at the wiry figure on the seat ahead of me. At the moment we were all crammed into a Volkswagen van, bumping along a dirt road to a Youth for Peace conference at the coast. It happened every year, right after Christmas. Kids came from all over the state. I always went. So did Jim. Neither of us had spoken since one of the conference leaders picked us up at the Greyhound depot in San Luis Obispo. I looked out the back window at the cloud of dust boiling up behind us.

Jim's hair was dark, with the faintest bit of wave. He kept it long enough to infuriate school officials, but just short enough so they couldn't make him do anything about it. His eyes were deep and blue, and used to gaze out like a summer ocean — but since he'd come to Sierra Vista, they'd been flat metal plates, hard, impenetrable. I hated him with a passion.

I'd known Jim — sort of — for years. But that counted for nothing after the summer of 1967 when the Vietnam war dealt Jim's family the same blow it dealt thousands and thousands of other families across the country. Maybe other families weren't rocked by explosions afterwards, or maybe they were. With Jim's case I was caught in the fallout.

Take a domineering father, a retired U.S. Marine Corps captain, veteran of Korea and World War II. Take an older brother, a really nice guy who had trouble saying no, even though that meant volunteering to fight in a war that he found morally abhorrent. Add a slightly younger brother who thought everything through with a ruthless clarity until he knew exactly where he stood, and didn't hesitate to stand up for what he believed in.

There were other players, a mother, and a younger sister and brother. I didn't hear as much about them. When Russell Holland Junior's unit was mistakenly ambushed by another unit from the same battalion in the central highlands of South Vietnam, James David Holland refused to live under the same roof as the man who'd bullied his eldest son to a senseless and violent death. And so he came to Sierra Vista to live with his maternal grandparents. Who happened to be our next-door neighbours.

The chemistry was bad from the start. Jim couldn't tolerate anybody feeling sorry for him. In spite of the fact that I admired the stance he'd taken, every time I tried to be friendly, he took it wrong. And so I regularly ended up putting my foot in my mouth, if you know what I mean. After a while I *did* quit feeling sorry for him. But the loss of his brother was something else altogether. I'd seen enough of Russ Holland at Youth for Peace conferences, and family visits to Sierra Vista, to be rather shaken up myself.

The other big reason it didn't work between Jim and me was that he took over my first chair trumpet position in band, meaning I got demoted. He was in most of my other classes, too. With him acting like a you-know-what, I got pretty bent out of shape. Soon we were both spitting fire and sabotaging each other's moves, while at the same time believing in peace and bringing an end to the Vietnam war.

The VW rounded the last bend, past gnarled oaks and solemn pines, and there was my friend Paula from Berkeley waiting by camp headquarters. Her red hair gleamed in the sunlight, a startling contrast to her purple granny skirt. "Kath!" she cried, as I jumped out.

I was engulfed in a flying bear hug. When I stepped back, I was dizzy from twirling. My friend's frizzy hair haloed her face; warm freckles spattered across her nose and cheeks, and I noticed that she wore dangly peace symbol earrings. A buoyant free feeling soared through me, such a change from the guilty, angry autumn. "Paula! It's good to see you!"

Her gold-brown eyes shone. "You too! C'mon, let's get your stuff up to the cabin. I saved you a place, but one of the San Francisco car pools is on its way and somebody might grab it."

The air smelled of pine and salt water. Suddenly I was laughing. Paula had that kind of effect on me. And the sunny coast was a far cry from the gloomy fog that closed in over the San Joaquin Valley every winter. I hiked my pack over my shoulder and ran up the bumpy path toward the girls' cabins.

Paula pushed ahead of me. We pounded up the wooden steps of *Yosemite* and stood there, panting. Different coloured sleeping bags were strewn across the floor. I flopped down, rolled out my bag too.

This conference was just what I needed. Forget the dull angry haze of school. True, Jim was here, but maybe I could put things in a better perspective. We'd all come to work at being peacemakers. Responsible world citizens. In past years it had all seemed intense and wonderful and loving, sort of like church, only a million times better. This time maybe I'd get some practical help.

Paula grinned at me. Then we went for a long walk on the beach. I told her everything.

* * * *

My cheeks were hot from a lot more than the blaze as I crouched in front of the huge stone fireplace in the main hall. Yet I scooted closer to the flames. With the poker I propped up a log that had fallen.

Sitting across from Jim Holland at supper was not my idea of wonderful. Despite good intentions.

It had been accidental, I was sure. He'd come in late and there probably weren't any other places. He hadn't done anything terrible. This time. But have you ever tried to eat while pretending the person opposite you really isn't there? I managed to sprinkle sugar on my peas and spill milk in my spaghetti and salad. He must've noticed. Extra points for him. Once we were done, Paula had to go straight to the kitchen for dishwashing crew, so I couldn't even talk to her.

Before me, splinters on the log surface crackled delicately. Tendrils of smoke rose when the hungry flames lapped them up. It was simplest to just sit, arms curled around my knees, and not think. Nearby, somebody was playing honky-tonk on an out-of-tune piano. He was really quite good. I could have enjoyed it, at a better time.

Paula emerged from the kitchen, hands red and puckered. "Snap out of it!" she ordered. "If things are as bad as you say, do you think he enjoyed sitting across from *you*? Besides," she went on, straightening her paisley skirt, "he still must be grieving. You have to make allowances for that."

That's what I'd thought, once. Later, when things started getting bad and I quit caring, I heard it from my mother. Often.

Rather than argue with Paula, I simply nodded and stared into the flames.

\* \* \* \*

Our conference dances were nothing like school dances, where girls got picked over like tomatoes at Super Valu, and the culls stood around trying to pretend they were groovy — or else ran off to cry in the can. At YFP we danced to ethnic folk tunes, not Beatles or Rolling Stones, or the dynamic Jefferson Airplane that could blast you into a whole different dimension. At YFP everybody danced, until you were so tired you could hardly stand up. Often you didn't need a partner, what with line dances and circle dances. Or if you did, it was no big deal to see girls dancing hand-in-hand or doing the good old *Allemande left, now SWING your partner, make her twirl* . . . Of course, it *was* more exciting if you ended up with a guy, and something like chemistry was happening . . .

\* \* \* \*

Accordion music blared from the record player. Paula kicked off her sandals and grabbed my hand. Circles materialized from the mob of kids standing around.

My feet moved automatically; my full dance skirt billowed out like a green sail. Happy faces flashed past. Laughter. Bare feet, even though it was winter. Jeans, often ragged, sometimes embroidered. Tie-dyed shirts. Peasant skirts and blouses like mine. The tension began to slip away.

Polkas. Feet light, body airy, though sweat trickled down my temples. Debkas, schottis-ches, horas. Square dances. A Russian troika sent some to the sidelines. I ignored the stabbing pain in my side like I ignored Jim Holland each time he swept by. But when the quiet beat of the Greek miserlou pulsed through the room, I mopped my face with relief.

Dancers flowed into lines. A hush whispered in the air; the lights dimmed. People became shadows as the last switch clicked, leaving only the orange flicker from the fireplace.

The lines of dancers fragmented, rejoined. I floated on the music, out the door to dance on the deck, was pulled back inside by the movement, by the gentle linking of hands. We wound through intricate patterns. United in the swaying motion, we were sisters and brothers, sharing a common humanity that stretched thousands of years back through time. When the final notes faded we stood there in silence, hands clasped.

Lights. It was inevitable. I blinked in the sudden brightness. A girl I didn't know stood at my right. On my left — Jim Holland. My neck muscles went rigid, marking the onset of a headache.

Jim recoiled, a faint shudder. Our hands parted.

Where was Paula?

Why didn't somebody put on another record?

Anything, to get out of *now*.

From the corner of my eye I glanced at him. His face was inscrutable. I couldn't just walk away. Everyone else stood there talking softly if at all. The same magic still held them, while I had frogs somersaulting in my stomach.

"Maybe it's about time we called a truce," he said.

What was the world coming to? My fingertips went icy. I pressed them against my clammy palms. "Maybe so." And after a tiny hesitation, "It's been pretty awful."

Silence. Off balance, I traced my foot along a floorboard and hoped I wouldn't

topple sideways. Especially not against him.
Jim wasn't pulling a disappearing act, so I
couldn't do it either. A refreshments table was
being set up. Soon I could escape without
being rude.

"Want some punch?" He sounded stilted.

A giddy image of a punch to his nose
triggered my nervous giggle. I stifled it, not
too successfully. "Okay." And then, because
he started across the room, I followed, feeling
like a U-Haul trailer. Why couldn't he be awful
as usual? Then I could leave and be mad.
Instead of scared half to death.

He gave me a paper cup of pink
lemonade. But my hand shook. I dropped it,
slopping some down my skirt, splatting the
rest across the floor. "Of all the stupid —!"
Face on fire, I knelt with a handful of napkins.
*Go away!* I screamed mentally. He did. But he
came back with paper towels. Once the spill
was cleaned up, I grabbed another cup and
escaped to the deck.

I gulped down the lemonade and stood
there in the night. The wind traced cool
fingers across my burning face. Still trembling, I picked at the paper cup, peeled it into
a spiral and then shredded that into long
dangling curlicues. In the room behind me
people were talking and laughing. I put my

head down on the rough cedar railing and listened to the heartbeat of the breakers in the distance.

"You're that scared of me?"

His voice startled me. The strips of paper slipped from my hand, white fluttering ribbons in the dark. "No." But it was a lie, and I knew he knew it.

He came out and leaned against the railing too.

I was so nervous I couldn't even think of dumb things to say. Silence vibrated between us. I couldn't turn and run; I'd already tried that, and he'd followed me. Inside, the kids milling around didn't seem real, not even Paula, who was sitting on the piano bench laughing up at some guy I didn't recognize.

"It must be good to be here," I stammered at last. "A change from everything — Sierra Vista, you know, and —" It sounded so idiotic I couldn't go on.

"It's hell," he said in a fierce, low voice.

I wished I could dissolve through the deck. Biting my lip, I jammed my toe into a knothole and waited.

"I hate it here." The explosive force in his voice made me jump. "All the little do-gooders who think they can actually accomplish something. Change the goddamn Establishment. What a load of crap."

"Then leave."

He glared at me as if I'd suggested he run away.

I scooted sideways, needing more space between us. "I remember Russ was here last year. He's —" I shook myself at my slip, forced more words out in a hurry. "He was a terrific volleyball player."

It would be heaven to walk away. But a truce would improve my quality of life considerably. I was hurting, too. I stood there thinking about Jim's older brother whose eyes had snapped with irresistible humour. Who'd accidentally spiked a volleyball right into my face — and when it turned out that I had a nosebleed, had left the game to sit with me until it stopped. It was outrageous and wrong that someone like that could be *gone,* no longer existing.

"Russell." Jim's voice suddenly was fragile. His knuckles were white above the railing.

A strange sense of wanting to touch him whispered through me, as if it could somehow help dissolve his pain. But I stood apart and said nothing.

Footsteps sounded in the doorway behind us. "Jim?" It was Carol McCutcheon, whose lilting soprano highlighted all our singalongs. "We're setting up for some music inside. Have you got your guitar?"

Jim went rigid beside me. His reply lashed out in words that were not repeatable.

A hot sweat broke out all over me. This was more like the Jim Holland I knew.

Carol's face contorted. "If that's how you feel, fine. I won't ask you again." She whirled around and strode back inside, brushing past a guy and girl who'd just wandered out to the deck.

Jim's fist slammed against the railing, which shuddered beneath my elbow. Then he dropped his head into both hands.

"Are you all right?" I asked after an uncomfortable silence. I kept my voice low so the couple would't hear. A quick glance reassured me; they were pretty wrapped up in themselves.

Jim didn't look up. "That was my girlfriend," he said with an ironic laugh. "Once. After the . . . funeral . . . she suddenly got allergic to me. Or something."

Tears blurred my eyes. It was a whole assortment of things. I couldn't even have explained to Paula. After a while, the pungent odour of marijuana drifted over in our direction.

Jim gave the kids a look of utter contempt. When he spoke again his voice was flippant. "Go ahead — go, Kath. That's what you really want to do, isn't it? I'm due for a meeting with the ocean, anyhow."

I tore through the room, not looking for Paula, and stumbled up the hill to the cabin. I burrowed into my sleeping bag, but that was too confining so I crashed through the brush and sat beneath the pine trees some distance away.

I stayed there a long time, ignoring the chatter of kids straggling back from the singing. An eternity later it was quiet.

The wind moaned through the needles overhead. In the distance I heard the deep bass thud of waves hitting cold sand. I shivered. But maybe I deserved to be cold.

How did it feel to lose your brother? Especially after such a terrible mistake. How did it feel to have a father you hated so much you couldn't stand living in the same house with him? I squirmed with shame at the petty nature of the feud between Jim and me. But maybe my reaction wasn't so different from Carol's. After all, she'd always seemed a nice person, not the type who'd play games with someone's feelings. Was it something about Jim, hurting so much he couldn't recognize other people's good intentions, only their weaknesses?

*A meeting with the ocean.* His words flickered like strobes in my mind. What on earth was that supposed to mean? Just a walk on the beach, or —?

I sat there, then lurched to my feet. My legs were all goosebumps, and stiff from being sat on too long. I skittered down the hairpin trail leading to the beach, my full skirt slapping against my legs. The salt air became a palpable moisture around me. High tide. The curling phosphorescent waves surged in, retreated in the moonlight as I slid with a spray of gravel down the last steep section of the trail.

I scanned the stretch of sand, alert for signs of movement. Nothing. I stared at the rocky expanse to the north, but didn't attempt it. In the dim light it was hard to tell the difference between rocks and their shadows. It would be too easy to fall and sprain an ankle. I called. Nothing. I called until I was hoarse. Still there was no answer.

Sick with worry and fatigue, I dragged myself back to the main hall. A few lights still burned. I went in, almost crying. In one corner somebody was picking at a guitar. It wasn't Jim.

Red embers were all that remained of the fire. I poked at them. Sparks sifted down, smothering into nothingness in the grey ash. The poker left a black smear on my hand. I rubbed my gritty eyes. Probably I'd streaked my face with soot, but so what? It was nothing, compared to . . .

I didn't have the nerve to go wake one of the adults. It was just a stupid worry, anyhow. I pulled one of the bulky over-stuffed chairs to the hearth and curled up in it, too tired and confused to think. Or sleep.

* * * *

Jim wasn't at breakfast. I told Paula about it over sticky oatmeal and soggy toast. She thought he'd probably just needed some time alone.

He wasn't in any of the discussion groups either. It was hard to concentrate. Then we saw an anti-war film. The blow-by-blow demonstration of how napalm worked left me so choked up with hopeless rage that I couldn't have talked to anybody even if I'd wanted to. So I perched on a fallen log in the wooded area.

A red glint caught my eye, a quick flash as I moved my hand. My school ring gathered the light and threw it back at me in red-and-gold echoes of the sun-shafts that filtered through the pines. I yanked the ring off, embarrassed, even though no one was there to see. I juggled it, stuffed it in my jeans pocket. School was just a make-believe world. It didn't teach you a thing about human misery. Or war.

A sparrow alighted nearby, small, dusky-brown with paler belly and flecked wingtips. I sat perfectly still. Its tiny head bobbed sideways, bright eyes unafraid. Breathlessly I willed it to come closer. It looked curiously at me. But my nose tickled. When I sneezed, the bird fluttered away.

Why did I have to wreck everything?

Everybody at the conference was talking about how to live a nonviolent lifestyle. Topics ranged from boycotting places that sold war toys to setting up draft counselling tables at school. Here I was, sucked right into the Establishment game. School rings. School spirit that caught at you, making you scream things out in excitement. Was that so different from what the Nazis had done in Germany? Or what the U.S. army was doing now, in boot camps? How could I claim to be a pacifist? After several months of hating Jim Holland so much that I'd even found myself wishing him bodily harm?

I couldn't sit still. My feet led me to the beach. The clean salt wind whipped my hair back from my face; the ocean danced with whitecaps.

The beach lay empty except for a couple heading away, trailing footprints in wet sand. I clambered over the blackish seaweed-covered rocks. The iodine odour of decaying vegetation rose to greet me; tiny insects swarmed up with every step, while the slippery plants popped beneath my feet.

I stopped at a large tidal pool and bent over to look at the creatures in the clear water. The fronds of a sea anemone drifted as I swished my finger past. A crab scuttled across the sandy bottom and disappeared beneath a rock shelf. One large orange starfish. Two smaller purple ones. I tapped my fingernail against the tightly clenched shell of a mussel. Limpets clung to rocks, looking like tiny submerged Chinese hats. Snails went about their business.

Slowly, miraculously, things began seeming all right again. These marine animals were living out their intended lives without pretense or conniving. Somehow we fit into the same scheme. But our understanding was imperfect. We made mistakes, sometimes caused real harm. Yet it seemed we could be forgiven.

Somebody was watching me. I sensed it just before the shadow fell across me. I straightened up.

Jim Holland stood there in a faded sweatshirt that said *Cal Berkeley* and a pair of holey jeans. His hair was windblown over a stubble-darkened face. He looked away the instant I turned, but I'd already seen the fatigue charcoaled beneath his eyes, the strain that coiled his features taut.

"Why'd you come looking for me last night?" he demanded.

I tensed. "Why didn't you answer?"

"I asked you first." His voice sounded dead.

I stood up and traced my toe in circles on a rock, then bent to tighten my laces. "I was worried," I admitted.

He laughed harshly. "*You?* Worry about me?"

I flinched, but made myself meet his mocking blue eyes. "You said something about a meeting with the ocean. I guess I got . . . scared." I clenched my teeth, so embarrassed I could scream.

"So you thought I was out here doing you a favour." His smile was ironic. "It *would* be a favour, wouldn't it."

My jaw dropped. But before I could protest, he went right on. "You'd have everything right back where it was. First chair in band. No competition, nobody to make you nervous every time you go in and out of your house. Nobody to mess up your life."

This was unbelievable. Impossible. *"Stop it!"* My foot stamped, and my fists clenched. "I thought you wanted a truce," I choked out, then turned away because there was no way I was letting him see me near tears.

"Truce. What a great word for it. Two antagonistic parties with missiles and atom bombs, and they call a truce so they won't blow each other up."

"Speak for yourself." The familiar black anger pulsed inside. The quiet dance. The time on the deck. It hadn't meant a thing. It was simply new weaponry for the same old war. How could I have been so naive?

"I usually do." He came to stand beside me, too close, propping one foot on a rock perched at the edge of the tidal pool.

I took a deliberate step away, putting more space between us. "What do you want? How come you keep following me around?"

Jim's foot wobbled the rock. "What do you *think* I want, the Humane Society picking me up like a stray dog?"

Suddenly I couldn't see straight. *"Get lost!"* My words spun out of control. "All you ever do is twist things around. Can't you get it through your stupid head that sometimes people *care*? It has nothing to do with pity. The way you treat everybody, I couldn't feel sorry for you if I tried."

"Another do-gooder." His blue eyes gleamed. "Push her too far and she'd rather do away with you instead." The rock wobbled again, fell with a hollow splash into the tidal pool.

I stared at the murky water where only moments ago sea anemones and starfish had been going about their quiet business. "You murderer! You've killed them!"

He gasped as if he'd been hit, but didn't strike back. When I finally dared look again, he was elbow deep in water but the rock hadn't moved. Sharp spasms were twisting his face. "You're so right," he said in that familiar bitter tone. But he was sobbing as he said it. "A murderer. I killed my brother."

"That's ridiculous." If things were different, I might've actually laughed. "The war killed him."

He heaved the rock out of the tidal pool, narrowly missing my foot. "A grenade killed him. An *American* grenade. But so did I. I bet you anything if I'd've kept quieter about the war . . . " He dropped his head into the crook of his elbow. "But no, I go and fight that fascist pig every chance I get — and so *he* starts getting on Russ's case, going after him like a tank until Russ drops out of university and joins up. That son-of-a-bitch." His voice broke down completely.

I knelt beside Jim and touched his shoulder. His sweatshirt was cool.

He shook my hand off. "What the hell do you care?"

I gulped in a steadying breath. "You're somebody I know, okay? And your brother was a really neat guy." I sniffled hard and put my arm around him.

He went stiff. "The bastard. Every day I want him dead. And some ways, I'm just *like* him." He shuddered, then collapsed into my lap.

Weeping, I held him to me. Steady, Kath. Love thy enemy. Love thy neighbour. Do unto others. I swallowed, told myself things. What do you do when someone you've hated is crying in your lap, so vulnerable you could smash his head with a rock? What *can* you do?

How can you keep hating him? When that person's pride — and yours — clash like swords, and then suddenly that pride falls?

I hung onto him, crying for him, for myself, wishing I could stamp out that horrible thing that was tearing him apart. I scooted closer so his head rested against my shoulder. I thought of my dad, so different from Jim's tyrannical parent. "Jim, it's not your fault." I said it over and over. There seemed nothing else to say.

He clung to me like a small child. Something inside me let go, forgetting I was Kathy Brady, forgetting everything except the tormented person who seemed to need me so badly. I held him close against me and still he cried as if it could never end.

Much later he quieted. My head rested against his; with an odd start I realized that I'd just kissed his upturned cheek. My hands played along his back in soothing, stroking motions. After a while he caught one of them and held it. Nearby the breakers kept surging in, hissing back out. It was like breathing. Like the new feelings that were creeping through me, terrifying in their clarity. Their intensity.

* * * *

I sat in a hollow between some rocks. Bemused, sore, not so scared anymore. My hair was tangled and matted. Sand had worked its way to my scalp. It was getting cold on the beach but I wasn't sure about going back.

Paula found me. She brought a sack lunch.

Her gold-brown eyes widened and she dropped to sit beside me. "Kath! What happened?"

My mouth opened but nothing came out. There wasn't anything that could possibly explain how I felt at being kissed like that. Or about the rest.

"Kath! Are you all right? What *happened*?"

"I — Jim — I . . ."

Gold-brown eyes flashed with an anger I hadn't known they were capable of. "Did he hurt you?" Silence. "Did he . . . rape you?"

I shook my head and raked my fingers through the sand. "I wanted to. But it was so intense." My voice cracked. "I'm scared, Paula."

She held me against her. "Was it your first time?"

I nodded.

She gave a little sigh but didn't speak.

"How can I love somebody like that if I hated him so much?"

She swayed, rocking me, rocking the both of us. "Strong emotions," she said at last. "Maybe it's all part of the same wiring."

I was inclined to agree. I wondered how Jim felt.

After a while Paula and I left the rocks. We built a giant sand castle, not talking much. We watched the waves roll in and swamp it. One of the turrets escaped undamaged.

* * * *

I didn't see Jim again until the next day. He sat alone on a hillside with his guitar. I didn't go close, but the breeze carried fragments of his music to me. I waved as I went by, slowly, but he gave no sign of having seen me.

The conference wound down to a bittersweet end. Jim did not appear at any of the meals or discussions. I caught a terrible cold, probably from too little sleep. On the last evening we had a bonfire on the beach, with singing and strumming guitars. Carol's sweet voice soared into the night as we sang our songs of peace.

I cried a lot that evening, but Paula was at my side so it was all right. Once I thought I saw Jim in the shadows some distance away. I willed him to come closer, but he vanished soon afterwards.

Paula saw him too. "I bet he still feels on the edge," she whispered by way of an explanation.

What about *me*? I wanted to scream. But everybody else was singing *Kum bah yah, my lord, kum bah yah* and my tennis shoes had been too close to the fire for too long, and were starting to smell like burnt rubber. I rested my head against my friend's shoulder and let the singing wash around me, comforting me, cleansing me.

Strong emotions. That was how we differed from the creatures in the tidal pool. Our job wasn't so easy. We could sure screw up if we weren't careful. But maybe part of it had to do with trusting. And accepting. Maybe that was what he'd really meant by . . . truce?

# BEGINNINGS

Eclipse was in town. A long time ago Tara and Curtis had planned to go to the concert. But that was a very long time ago. Now everything had changed.

She felt heavy. Swollen. Puffy. Nine months pregnant was not a comfortable way to feel. At least the baby had dropped and she could catch her breath more easily — but now the bulk made her waddle. Like an overweight duck. Curtis had no use for an overweight duck. Not even a pregnant girlfriend. It was a long time since she'd talked to him.

The scariest part was knowing that any time now that bulk would force its way out of her body.

"How's it going, little sister?"

Tara jumped as Karin breezed into the back yard. Slim. Tanned. Moving easily. It was impossible to repress the envy, but Tara looked up at her older sister with relief. "I feel like a duck," she announced.

Karin pulled up another lawn chair. "Well, you haven't grown any feathers yet. I wouldn't worry."

The baby kicked. Tara watched her stomach jiggle with its movement. Strange to think there was a person living inside her. "Okay," she retorted. "So I'm a statistic instead. Almost seventeen. Completed grade eleven. Registered for the program for teen mothers in the fall."

"Summer's a yukky time to be pregnant," Karin said.

"Tell me about it."

"I think we'll plan our next one to arrive in the spring."

*We. Plan.* The words stung. Even though Tara knew her sister hadn't intended them to, she couldn't control the flare of resentment. "You don't need to do it for *my* benefit. You guys can plan it for January, for all I care."

"Sorry." Karin lifted Tara's hair off her hot neck. "I know it's hard on you, kid. I didn't mean to be a pain."

*Well you are,* Tara felt like saying. But she curbed the impulse. Of all the people around her, Karin was the one who hadn't backed off. Mom had suddenly become the prickly martyr. Dad? He was in B.C. somewhere, and if he knew she was pregnant, she sure hadn't heard about it. Leah and Holly were sympathetic and more curious than they dared admit, but didn't understand, not at all. And Curtis? Worthless jerk! Good old Karin. She was the one who'd come to the prenatal classes with her, who'd helped her practice the breathing exercises. Karin would be there with her, day or night, whenever the baby decided to come.

"What do you say we go have a milkshake?" Karin went on. "I bet you haven't left this house for a week."

"Not since my last doctor's appointment," Tara admitted. "It doesn't matter." She stared at a patch of grass as if it suddenly had become very interesting. Actually, it was full of chickweed.

"Come *on!* You're acting like an old woman."

"Old women can't get pregnant."

"That's not the point. There must be *something* you feel like doing."

"Eclipse is in town," Tara said wistfully. "But the tickets sold out two months ago."

"Shoot. It would've been fun to go." Karin dropped her chin into her hands. The sun gleamed off her caramel-blonde hair and her slim tanned legs.

"Where's D'Arcy?" Tara asked. Usually her thirteen-month-old niece went everywhere with Karin.

Karin grinned. "Sleeping. At her Grandma Olson's. Actually, Duane's mom offered to take her for the whole afternoon. I'm *free,* little sister. So let's go do something!"

Tara sat there. The baby wiggled. Then came a familiar tightening within. The doctor had a name for those contractions, but she couldn't remember what it was. He said they were perfectly normal, and happened more frequently toward the end of pregnancy. Tara put her hand on her rounded belly and rubbed, breathing carefully.

"You okay, sis?" Karin's thoughtful hazel eyes were studying her.

It was gone. "Yeah," Tara said, relieved. "One of those spasms."

"Oh yeah. Braxton Hicks. They can get a little sharp towards the end." Karin grabbed Tara's wrists and pulled. "Up, young woman! I just had the most awesome idea. It's exactly what the doctor ordered, for you and me both."

"What?" A lot of Karin's ideas involved being active, and that was *not* what she wanted.

"Stand up, nitwit! You're all out of joint because of that concert, right? And it makes you think about that twit who helped get you in this condition, right? Go grab all your Eclipse tapes. We'll go out to the lake and have our own concert, in the cottage."

It was much easier getting her bulk out of the chair with her sister's help. Tara stood up. A robin on the grass paused in its hunt for food and carefully looked at her, first with one eye, then the other.

The lake. What an all-right idea! It never seemed as hot at the lake. The people there were more relaxed and less likely to glare at you if they were in a hurry and you weren't. Tapes. The cottage. She and Karin could really crank up the volume on Karin's boom box. Karin would dance, for sure. It might actually be fun.

"Okay," she said. She waddled along beside her sister, then waited while Karin wrote the note for their mother to find when she got off work.

It was great to be on the highway, with Eclipse pulsing from the rear speakers. The wheatfields were turning golden, and all that open space made Tara feel as though she could breathe again. Clouds were building up in the west. Maybe there'd be a storm. That wouldn't be half bad; it'd clear out the heat. Tara opened her window all the way so the wind could roar around her.

"Hey!" Karin yelled. "You're blowing my hair in my face." She didn't sound terribly upset so Tara reached in her duffel bag for an elastic and captured her sister's flyaway hair. Karin grinned at her. "Thanks." She flicked on the headlights. "The lights're on, Duane," she announced. "Silly guy's been on my case lately — *Use the headlights when you're on the highway, Karin.*" She tapped her fingertips against the steering wheel. "You're my witness, okay?"

"Okay." Tara sucked in a deep breath as another spasm caught her. It would be a relief to have all of this over with. On the other hand, the thought of motherhood still terrified her. The tiny sleepers and bibs and receiving blankets that were slowly accumulating in her bottom dresser drawer did little to reassure her.

"*– come with me . . . for our ne-ext beginning . . .*"

Tara closed her eyes and sang along while the wind played with her hair. She opened them much later as the car slowed way down and gravel spat against its underside. The lake lay before them, a calm reflective blue reaching in both directions. Tara sighed. She felt cooler already.

The tape ended. She popped it out of the player as Karin pulled into the narrow drive. Tara maneuvered her way out of the car and stood knee-deep in a patch of yellow clover and thistle.

"So," said Karin. "Want to go inside and have our concert, or get a look at the lake first?"

"Go to the beach," Tara said, surprising herself. She tossed her duffel bag over her shoulder and got Karin's boom box from the trunk while her sister wrestled with a bag full of eats. A spasm caught her as she stepped onto the unpainted wooden verandah. She winced, and set everything down inside the cottage.

As they walked down the gravel roadway, Tara could see that Karin was deliberately slowing her usually bouncy pace. Back to duck mode, she thought. Or maybe cow. Her breasts were very sore. Her feet, in runners, kicked gravel. A larger-than-usual chunk pelted into Macgregors' flower bed, levelling a couple of daisies. Guiltily, she looked to see whether their closest neighbours at the lake had noticed. But the windows of the cottage

were boarded up and no car was in sight. Tara
relaxed and kicked more gravel.

There weren't terribly many people at the
beach. Perhaps it was due to the coming
storm. Tara looked at the clouds and then
shed her shoes. The water was slapping at the
shore in inviting little splashes. Already she
could feel its coolness soothing her swollen
ankles and puffy legs. She started across the
sand and discovered she could hardly walk
because of her monstrously oversized belly.

Tears stung her eyes. She wasn't just a
cow, she was a stupid clumsy uncoordinated
*old* cow who could only stagger about.

"Don't worry, kid." Karin was at her
elbow, helping propel her along. "I got like
this last year, remember?"

Suddenly she *did* remember. She also
remembered how she'd laughed at Karin, and
how Karin had made a huge show of pretending to be a beached whale until Duane picked
her up and carried her to the water.

A sharp tightness gripped her lower
abdomen. Tara gasped and put her hand to
the spot.

Karin stopped walking. "You okay, sis?"

"Yeah," she said doggedly.

Karin seemed to be weighing something
in her mind. She looked at the bank of clouds,

across the lake, up at the road. "You've had quite a few of those, haven't you," she said at last.

Tara tensed. No. It couldn't be. She wasn't ready. "Not much different from the last couple of days," she said. It wasn't exactly true, but suddenly more than anything she needed to be at the lake. It was beautiful. Unspoiled. She took in a deep breath of water-scented air. If anything could fix the way she'd been feeling, it was the lake, with Karin there too.

Karin relaxed visibly and guided her down to the water. "It'll be any day now, I bet," she said.

At first touch the water had a cold bite, but right away Tara was used to it. She took another deep breath and relaxed with the cool, sloshing movement. A small sailboat with a yellow-and-red sail was sweeping steadily along the opposite shore. Further north, a power boat and water skier were chopping across the surface. The boat approached, then passed; its wake slapped about her knees.

"Have you decided on a name yet?"

Tara curled her toes around a pebble. "Kayla. Kayla Ann."

"I know you like *that* one." There was a hint of dry humour in her sister's voice. "What if it's a boy?"

Tara brushed her hair back from her shoulders and gave her older sister a mock-scowl. "I'm having a girl. So there."

"And if you don't?"

"Oh, probably Horace or Quigley or something." She giggled. For the past few months she'd had no use for the male sex.

"Get serious, will you? You're running out of time."

Tara glared at her. "I can hardly call it Curtis, can I? Or what about Donald, after Dad. Some lot of good he's doing us."

The breeze stilled as the dark clouds rolled in with a stern authority. Tara looked up at them. They were absolutely humongous, with nervous sullen bases topped by massive grey-white pillars. They looked like sculptures whose tops had been flattened and squished forward by some huge, unseen hand.

"I don't think I like the looks of that sky," Karin said.

"We can't go in *yet.*" Tara tunnelled her feet into the sand. The movement of the water around her was so soothing. But the lower end of the lake had gone from its clear pale blue to a flat, dark metal colour.

A streak of lightning zapped to earth somewhere beyond the western shore. The roll of thunder blundered across the sky, reminding Tara of the tympani when she'd still played in the band.

"I don't like it." Karin's voice was nervous. She'd always been frightened of thunderstorms. "Look at that. I think we should go in."

Tara followed her sister's pointing arm. Further west the sky was taking on a poisonous green-grey cast. As she watched, the clouds swallowed the sun. Colour was bleached from the lake, from the trees, even from Karin's bright orange T-shirt. Directly overhead the sky was still blue, but it was an eerie flat blue, more like cheap paint than the living colour that the sky was supposed to be. And all around them the treetops were absolutely still. Tara shivered. "Okay," she said.

"I hope you feel like running," Karin muttered.

"Hah." But she tried to hurry her heavy self as her sister tugged her across the difficult sand and then up the gravel road. Soon the clouds had claimed the entire sky, bringing a murky late-evening darkness. Lightning forked too often for comfort and the thunder almost seemed to blast leaves off the trees.

Rain began pelting down just before they reached the cottage, huge cold splats which at first sent puffs of dust scurrying upwards, and moments later sluiced down in a grey screen. Tara ducked away from it, hugging her cold wet belly.

"Whew!" Karin gasped as she slammed the cottage door behind them. "A nasty one!"

Tara sagged into the soft-cushioned wicker chair. The baby was writhing around inside as if it were terrified.

The realization jolted her. She breathed slowly and deeply and began massaging the huge round lump. "It's all right, little guy," she said softly. It felt like the right thing to do, and so she said it over and over again. She almost didn't notice when her sister turned on the music.

Karin beckoned. "Come on, sister, let's dance!"

She was reluctant to get up and break the mood which held her. For almost her entire pregnancy she'd hardly thought of the baby as a person who had needs. But it *was*, and soon it would be up to her to understand, and know what to do.

Karin beckoned again. "Come on! You may not get another chance for a *long* time."

So with Eclipse booming through the speakers, constantly interrupted by thunder, and rain pouring down so hard she halfway thought the roof would cave in, Tara got up.

Her bulky body wasn't accustomed to dancing. Every now and then her abdomen would pull her off balance. The sharp spasms didn't help either. The lights flickered under the onslaught of the storm. And outside, through the dense curtain of rain, Tara could see that the wind had returned and was whipping treetops as casually as if they were the petunias in her mother's flowerbed.

And then the strongest spasm yet bent her double. Tara squeezed her eyes shut and tried to breathe deeply, into the pain, in order to relax the incredible knot of tension there. She backed up to a chair and as she sat, a warm gush of fluid splashed down her legs.

She sat there stunned, caught in a web of noise. "Kare!" she gasped. "Turn off the tape!"

Eclipse was silenced, but not the storm. The cottage shuddered with each boom of thunder, with every strong gust of wind. Tara sat there in the chair and couldn't think. Suddenly she felt numb all over.

Karin's face went white. "Oh my God, you're in labour!" She paced over to a window, flinching as the surreal cast of lightning flooded the room. "So now I get to drive you home in this." Tara watched as her sister clung to the windowsill and moaned, "Why, dear Mother, didn't you ever put a phone in this place?"

So this was it. A mosquito of fear was whining about her, but it didn't seem able to get past the numb feeling. Now she'd find out how the big thing inside her would work its way out. Another contraction caught her. *Breathe,* she reminded herself, hearing the voice of the public health nurse at the prenatal class.

"Sometimes it helps if you walk around," Karin said. "I'll go on out and start the car." The door opened and her sister disappeared into the storm.

Tara pushed herself up and walked around the perimeter of the small living room. It felt good to be here, amidst all the things she'd known since she and Karin were little. Things that her mother had used when *she* was a girl. It made her feel safe, even as a deafening roll of thunder left her cowering. Some of the furniture was incredibly old fashioned. From the fifties, her mother said. She looked at a chipped white enamel pitcher on a shelf in the kitchen. Mom said Grandma O'Brien had been given that pitcher as a

wedding present. Ages ago. And now —
Another painful contraction gripped her
whole lower self. Tara breathed carefully and
massaged her belly. What was taking Karin so
long?

Then her sister was standing in the doorway, drenched to the skin and looking limp
with dread. "I left the lights on," she said dully.
"The car won't start."

Tara's mouth dropped open. The hover-
ing fear found its way in. "Oh no!" she wailed.
To be stuck *here*, having a baby? With no
doctors or nurses, not even Mom? No
telephone. No car. No neighbours to run to,
and the storm so bad it would be dangerous
to go further down the road in search of help.

Karin grasped her shoulders. "Tara, don't
lose it. Everything's going to be *all right.*"

Tara nodded, wanting to believe her
sister's words. But — *this just couldn't be
happening!* She clutched her rounded belly
which now controlled her with a life of its own,
and wished she could miraculously stop
everything.

"Come on." Karin led her over to the
couch and then turned the tape on again, but
not quite so loud. "Relax. At least the power's
not out, and this storm isn't going to last
forever. Babies take a while to come.

Remember, in your class they said the average labour for a first pregnancy is something like eleven hours."

Tara nodded again. It hadn't taken that long for D'Arcy to arrive, though. She didn't know exactly how many hours it had been, but every now and then Karin still laughed about how she'd barely made it to the hospital in time. When had these contractions started? In the lawn chair, in the back yard? That was already something like three hours ago. Another one gripped her. It was uncomfortable sitting there on the couch.

Karin noticed. "Walk around," she advised. "It'll help take your mind off things. Or, what the heck — dance, why don't you? That's what we came here to do."

A strange giddiness grasped Tara. She walked over to the boom box and turned the volume way up. The familiar voices of Eclipse belted into the air, penetrating her skin.

"Hey!" She could hardly hear her sister's voice. "Trying to make us deaf or something?"

Tara grinned. With the music so loud around her the thunderstorm was just background noise. She danced. Every few minutes she had to stop for a contraction.

*"Breathe!"* Karin yelled right in her face during a long, painful one.

It hurt to breathe. Tara thought back to all the breathing practice, and began to pant. It seemed to help. But a steady feeling of pressure was bothering her. She went to use the washroom, but it didn't help. Several more tries did no good either. Her stomach was beginning to feel a little sick, and a sweat broke out in pinpoints all over her face and neck. She curled up on the couch.

"You okay, sis?" Karin shouted, and turned the volume down.

She shook her head. "I don't feel so good."

Her sister stroked her forehead. "Poor kid. Take it easy, okay?"

Karin's hand felt so good. Tara tried to relax, but the queasy feeling continued. So did the pressure. And the contractions were beginning to feel different. It was as if all of her lower insides were being compressed by a giant clamp. "I feel like I have to push!" she gasped in the midst of a severe one.

Karin didn't say anything. But her hand suddenly was icy.

Outside, the claps of thunder weren't quite so loud or frequent, though the rain continued hammering down.

"Karin!" Tara tugged at her sister's arm. "I feel like I have to push. Doesn't that mean –"

Karin's mouth tightened into a line. She shook her hair back from her face. "Could be, sis. Maybe I should take a run down the road to find someone who has a phone."

Logically Tara knew that was best. But she couldn't seem to let go of her sister's arm. "Don't go!" she begged. Another contraction set in. She bore down with it.

Karin's hazel eyes looked like those of a trapped animal. "Women have been having babies for millions of years," she said in a rush. "You're healthy, the baby's healthy. Everything's going to be *fine*. I won't be gone long. Promise."

She was gone. Emptiness filled the cottage. Tara lay there on her side, on the couch, and cried. Karin had called her a woman. But she didn't feel like any woman. A little girl was more like it. Lost. Abandoned. Again. The terrifying alien force that was acting upon her body was too much to face alone. Something inside her wanted to scream. She clenched her teeth and breathed deeply instead. If she lost control it would be a total zoo.

She waited, staring blankly at the low bookcase that sat beneath the window, while lightning ricocheted across the sky. She breathed. She pushed. The contractions hurt so much it was hard to keep from being swallowed by the pain. She cried.

She had no idea how much time passed before the door burst open. Suddenly Karin was beside her, holding her hand and stroking her forehead. "Sorry it took so long," she panted. "A lot of places are locked up. But Herbisons' wasn't, so I went on in and called the RCMP. They said it might take a little while. There was a tornado over at Muddy Flats, and it dropped somebody's roof on the road between here and there."

Tara let out a moan. She squeezed Karin's hand as another contraction began. They were lasting much longer now. The public health nurse and all of Karin's coaching practice were fuzzy and too far away to remember.

"Don't panic." Karin's voice cut in. "You're doing just great, Tara. Hold your breath and push with the contraction. Push. *Hard.* Come on, you can do it!"

"I can't!" she wailed.

"Yes you can. Probably only another forty-five seconds before this one's gone. I did it having D'Arcy. So can you. Come on, sis, *push.* You're doing just great."

Tara's teeth gritted. She strained forward, pushing as hard as she could. A wild cry burst out of her, while another part of her stood back in amazement. Then it was gone.

"Good girl." Karin's voice. "I'll be back in just a sec. Rest. Then we'll see about getting you in a better position."

She closed her eyes and breathed deeply. A moment later a cool damp cloth was wiping her face. It felt so good. "Kare," she gasped. "I'm feeling that burning sensation they talked about in class. Does that mean —?"

She heard her sister's sharp intake of breath. "I'll go start water boiling," Karin said after a long silent moment.

Push.

Wait.

Push.

Wait.

It went on and on, until her awareness could no longer reach beyond what was happening in her body. The burning sensation grew stronger, stronger . . . Pushing so hard she was afraid she'd explode; strange animal sounds coming from her . . . And then there suddenly was a *pop* and an immense feeling of relief.

"The head's out." Karin's voice was shaky. "Breathe, sis. On the next one, your kid'll be here. Have a look if you want."

She breathed obediently. It would be good for her, good for the baby, too. The baby . . . Trembling, Tara curled herself forward and saw the baby's head reaching out of her. It looked like a big doll's head, all messy with blood. She felt positively unreal.

Karin squeezed her hands. "I've got to go find a couple more things. Don't worry, sis. For you, the worst is over. Yell when the next one starts."

In this bizarre state, she suddenly realized how terrified her sister must be. It wasn't like Karin was a nurse or a paramedic. The only training she'd had was giving birth to D'Arcy, and the prenatal classes. Tara wanted to say something to her, but she was so tired she couldn't think. Her hand reached and stroked the baby's slippery wet head. "Hi, kid," she said.

The contraction came. She made a sound, and Karin was there. "Don't push this time," she ordered. Tara obeyed. The baby slid out into her sister's waiting hands.

"It's a boy," Karin said. She bent over the baby, wiping its face or something, and Tara couldn't see. She held her breath. A moment later there was a strange raspy cry.

Tara relaxed. But . . . a boy? How could it be?

But then her sister held out the tiny squalling little boy. His entire body was red and his little face was screwed up, eyes squeezed shut, and he was screaming in panic. "Go on," said Karin. "Hold your kid. He won't break. And he needs you more than he needs me."

Tara looked at the baby. Something heaved in her chest. She could love this little boy. Trembling, she reached for him. "What do I do with him?"

"Put him to nurse. Or lay him on your tummy. He's gotta be kept warm. And I have to figure out how to do the cord. I remember with D'Arcy they clamped it in two places . . . " Karin sounded totally distracted.

He was so tiny, so helpless, and still attached to the long purple cord that disappeared inside her. "Hi, guy," she said to her baby. "I'm your mom." With a fingertip she stroked his forehead. He kept on yelling. His lungs seemed to be working just fine.

Warm. He needed to be kept warm. She placed him on her belly, which was soft and puffy now like a deflating balloon, and covered him with the towels that Karin handed to her. The crying stopped.

"Hi," she said again. "What's your name, little guy?"

One eye slowly opened, a slatey blue-grey. He looked totally bewildered. Just as slowly, his other eye opened.

She lay there looking at her baby as the afterbirth slithered out. He was so fascinating she didn't think she'd ever be able to stop looking at him.

"Whew!" Karin said several minutes later. "I don't know what the heck I'm supposed to be doing, but as far as I can tell, everything's okay." Tara heard the sound of the kitchen tap running. Then Karin reappeared. "Now, let's get a look at the little guy." She bent forward. "Know what? I think he looks a lot like you, sis. I remember exactly how you looked when they brought you home."

The baby gave a delicate yawn and suddenly was asleep. Tara gently touched his tiny ears, his little bud of a nose, his incredibly soft cheeks; she stroked his little back. At last she tore herself away. "Isn't he *incredible?*" she said to Karin. She was so choked up she could hardly speak.

"He sure is." Karin bent and gave her a kiss on the forehead. "And so are you."

After all that hard work she was feeling sort of woozy herself. "His name's Carey," she announced, wanting to share the stunned glow of warmth inside.

Her sister understood. Tears came to her eyes and she sniffled audibly.

Carey Sullivan. It sounded pretty good. And maybe Thomas for his middle name, after Grandad O'Brien. That worked, Carey Thomas Sullivan. But there'd be plenty of time to think about that later. An RCMP officer had just walked past the front window. Footsteps thudded on the verandah.

Tara reached for a blanket to cover herself. Her baby jerked at the movement and cried. Cautiously she picked him up. "It's okay, Carey," she murmured. She put him to her breast. His tiny mouth fumbled around and then suddenly figured out what to do. It felt totally awesome.

Beginnings. Everything was beginnings. Everything was beginning for Carey. *Carey* was a beginning. She was a mother, and she had a lot to learn.

A loud knock came at the door.

# AFTERWORD

Ideas for stories come from many different places. Often they are slow to come, bits and pieces of happenings which tumble about, rubbing against one another, and which may or may not develop into a workable story. A few stories, on the other hand, are "gifts" whose origins can be traced to an exact moment.

"Of Time and Teeth" is such a gift. In 1971 I worked for a few weeks as a "casual" nurse's aide in a private hospital not unlike Blenkinsop Manor. One day elderly Mrs. K. turned to me and said, "I'll be dead tomorra." I never went back to work there, as I got a full-time job — yet I was left forever wondering just what had happened. Thirteen years later the story revealed itself in a flash, and I wrote it.

"The Michelle I Know" is written in memory of Tony, a teacher very sick with leukemia, who used to play his guitar in Fresno Community Hospital where my first husband was also a cancer patient for a time. Tony taught me the Spanish words to a few songs that I liked.

"Laws of E/motion" comes from a private and very painful time when my husband was gravely ill, with fond thoughts for Helen, my mother-in-law, who flew to Saskatchewan in the dead of winter to be with us, and who shared my grief.

Not all of the stories had sad beginnings. The first version of "To Touch a Shadow" was written two years after a long-distance visit from a boyfriend I didn't want to be visited by. But the story didn't really come together until fourteen years later, when I thought it would be much more fun if I wrote about a guy I'd met at music camp later that same summer, only nothing happened . . . (Drat!) There really was an irrigation ditch along the boundary of my parents' five acres in Reedley, California. As much as anything, this story is to help commemorate that ditch, now channelled through underground pipes, and all the orchards and vineyards that have been torn down for subdivisions.

My high school band teacher doesn't know this, but "It Wasn't My Fault" is a gift from him. Sixteen years after graduation, I was in town for a while and took my son to a football game one Friday night. It started raining . . .

The second-to-last time I went to Santa Monica Beach before moving to Canada in 1971, I saw a genuine red tide. It was freaky, to say the least, and I always knew I'd write about it someday. The trouble was, it took 21 years to find the story!

For the longest time, "Truce" was a turning-point chapter in a 1960s novel that New York publishers kept liking, but never buying. Finally, in frustration at wanting a "new" story to enter in a competition, I lifted the chapter and changed the end. This one is for Kathy (*not* the "I" of the story) who read many drafts, and always gave me helpful comments.

"Something About that Girl" is for Josef. Ever since my first book *Who Cares About Karen?* was published in 1983, he has been wanting to read more about Karen.

Except . . . this one turned out to be more about Stan.

My first husband had a 1961 VW Beetle when I met him; when we bought a new car in 1970, guess which one I ended up driving.

"One Wasted Saturday" came as a result of a persistent image which kept crossing my mind during lengthy hospital visits in 1985, the image of a stranded car, with the only person able (or perhaps *not* able) to go for help being a paraplegic kid.

And finally, as a teenager I had a burning curiosity about how it felt to have a baby — except, it was *never* in books, and none of the adults I knew ever talked about it in any detail. So I went ahead and wrote this story, once I knew what it felt like. It just seemed that it would be more interesting if there was no hospital nearby . . .